[Euphoria Kids]

Euphoria Kids

ALISON EVANS

echo

Echo Publishing
An imprint of Bonnier Books UK
80-81 Wimpole Street
London W1G 9RE
www.echopublishing.com.au
www.bonnierbooks.co.uk

First published 2020

Cover design by Jem Bradbrook and Jo Hunt
Page design and typesetting by Shaun Jury

Typeset in Electra LT

Printed in Australia at Griffin Press.
Only wood grown from sustainable regrowth forests is used in the
manufacture of paper found in this book.

NATIONAL
LIBRARY
OF AUSTRALIA

A catalogue record for this book is available from the National
Library of Australia
ISBN: 9781760685850 (paperback)
ISBN: 9781760686499 (ebook)

echopublishingaustralia

echo_publishing

echo_publishing

Dear reader,

I write these stories because I can't get the fifteen year old me out of my head, the one who was so scared because they thought that they were alone. I don't want anyone else to feel that.

I want people to know about gender euphoria. I want them to learn about it before gender dysphoria. I want the young trans kids that will read this book to be proud of who they are, and imagine wonderful, magic lives for themselves.

Alison Evans
23/10/2019

Contents

Chapter One
The Plant Child

B efore the rose was there, the garden was full of moss. I started as a seed under it, waiting for the right time to sprout. Clover waited, and waited, and tended the garden, and didn't listen to anyone who said she should give up. Moss, my other mother, she waited too. But Clover was the one who came out every morning and told me about her night, what she was planning on cooking that day, how Moss was going.

On the first day of spring, I thought it was the right time. Clover did too, I think; the day before, she'd whispered through the ground that she knew I'd be there soon.

When my first two leaves emerged, Moss and Clover knew I would be okay.

I didn't mean to be a strange baby made of plants, but it hasn't caused any problems. I don't know if anyone else can tell. Only Clover and Moss talk about it.

After I emerged from the ground, Clover fertilised the garden bed and made a home for the rosebush with its moon flowers. Now it's as tall as me.

Saltkin flits over and touches a closed bud, waiting for its time. 'Look at this, Iris.' He beckons me closer. I have to squint to see him in the almost-dawn. He's changed his skin – now he's a tiny fat boy and he's kept his wings.

'Your spring look?'

'Maybe. Not sure on the colour scheme.' He preens one of his bright-green iridescent wings with his fingers.

'You look good.'

He smiles and moves to sit on my raised hand, crossing his legs. He's the weight of a bird. 'Are you going to change?'

'You know I can't change like you.' I wave my free hand around, and he flutters so he's hovering in front of my face like a hummingbird. 'It's different for me.'

'I meant, you know. Like your hair. Or get some metal in your face. You love tattoos, you could get some of those.'

'I'm too young for tattoos,' I say. I want to cover my body in art and stories, watch them move and flex as I go through the days. I want to cover my body in flowers and vines. But not for a couple of years.

'We can do something with your hair,' Saltkin says, touching a bit of it that's fallen out of my ponytail. 'You'd look nice pink.'

'Why don't you go pink? Keep the green wings, though.'

He closes his eyes and the snow-blue of him changes to a peachy pink, with patches of orange.

'You look like a rose,' I tell him.

There's so much potential in winter, and the very beginning of spring is my favourite. Anything could happen. The world is waking up again, and even now, in the dark backyard, the air is humming with new energy.

A couple of other faeries who I've seen before but don't know well come over and speak to Saltkin. I can't understand what they're saying; it sounds like music.

I walk around the garden. Clover tends it; sometimes I help, but she is the reason it thrives. She grows us vegetables and herbs, and when flowers are blooming, there are always some in vases in the kitchen.

The rosemary bush has been here since long before Clover and Moss moved in, and when we're gone it will take over the whole backyard. I pinch off a stalk and, leaving Saltkin to his friends, I return to the house. The back door leads right into the kitchen. I switch on the kettle, and as it starts to boil the kitchen starts to awaken. The tiles are different patterns but all various shades of green and blue, salvaged from seconds bins and the tip. The benches are a dark wood, stained with years of cooking and spillages. I put the rosemary sprig in a thin glass vase and place it on the windowsill, its scent lingering on my hands.

The yellow overhead light flickers on, and Clover is there when I turn around, sitting, still blurry-eyed. I hug her good morning. 'You're up early,' she says. She always gets up at this time.

'It's spring.'

'Oh.' She looks through the window, though it's still too dark to see outside now the light is on. 'Of course.'

I always wake up early on the first day of spring.

I make us a pot of rooibos tea and sit opposite her as it brews. She spoons honey into our cups. As she pours the tea, I ask, 'What are you doing today?'

'Moss has the day off. We're just going to hang about, I think. Do you want a lift to school?'

I think of Saltkin and his fae friends, and how my mothers have each other. I know lots of creatures, and I have my mothers, but I don't have my own people.

'I don't mind catching the bus. I like the walk.' It's not long, maybe five minutes. Sometimes the stop is right outside the house; I'm not sure what that depends on, exactly.

There are still a couple of hours before I have to go to school, and so I take the half-drunk tea to my room and get back into bed. The sun is rising, soft light covering the garden. I can see the glitter that is Saltkin and the others, and I feel a tiny bit of annoyance.

Just like that, he appears on my windowsill. 'Sorry, Iris,' he says, pausing at the sill to see if I'll tell him to go away. Sometimes I do. It's hard to get privacy when you're friends with faeries. 'Are you mad?'

'A little.' I sip the tea and beckon him to sit on my bed. 'But I don't know if that's fair. I think I'm jealous of you.'

'The magic?'

'The friends. I don't have any.' I'm envious of the magic, too, but we've been over that.

'We're not friends?' I can tell I've hurt him.

'Sorry, I don't mean we're not friends. I mean, I need human friends.'

He still looks a bit put out, and I feel like I would be too.

'Like how Clover has Moss. They understand each other, and they're in love but they're friends too. And your other friends near the rosebush. You have a connection with them that we can't have.'

He nods. 'I'll be right back.' He flits out the window, and I stare after him for maybe five minutes before I wonder if he's not coming back. My tea has gone cold, so I lie back down. I set my phone alarm just in case I fall asleep and miss the bus.

When I wake for the second time that morning, herbs, flowers and rocks are strewn all over the bed. I reach for the closest one, a rose quartz. It's polished smooth but it's not quite perfectly round, like it's been sitting on a riverbed for a long time.

There is a tiny note on the bedside table. *A spell for friends* is written in loopy, thin, spindly letters. I've never seen Saltkin's handwriting before, but I assume it's from him.

My alarm goes off and I get out of bed, trying my

best not to disturb the debris on the covers. I pull on my uniform, in varying shades of blue, and pocket the rose quartz. The bus stop takes me twice as long to walk to today, and by the time I reach it I'm sweating.

There is a new person on the bus wearing our uniform. I've memorised all the faces that get on, and what stops they belong to. But theirs is new.

They've got straight black hair, cut so it's just shorter than their chin. They're wearing a choker, just a thin black one with a silver star on it. They're wearing a smidge of eyeshadow, not enough for a teacher to tell them not to. Their uniform is frayed a bit, so they might not be new. There's a denim jacket on the seat beside them.

They look at me, catch me looking at them, and I quickly look away. My cheeks are burning as I stare at the scenery rushing past. We go through ten minutes of bush before we get to the town, and the school.

In science, that's when I notice they're in my year. The new person. But no one is really paying them any attention. We're paired together because I have no friends and everyone else is paired up.

'Are you new?' I ask. They seem like they're not; they don't look lost. Up close, their dress is patched in a couple of places, definitely an old uniform.

'No.' They smile at me. 'But you probably just haven't noticed me. I'm Babs.'

'Iris.'

'Like the song?'

I look at them blankly.

'You know. Goo Goo Dolls?'

'Oh.' I pause. 'My mums chose my name. But it's a good song.'

'I chose my name,' they say. 'I just liked the sound. I like how it makes me sound like an old lady.'

We smile at each other. We fill out the sheet our teacher gave us, and then the bell rings, and we have different classes to go to. I think about asking them if they want to meet up later, but by the time I work up the courage, they're gone.

The next class I have is IT, but because we're on the computers no one's doing any work except me; I like to finish it early because then I won't have to do all of it the night before assignments are due. And today I'm glad to have some extra time. The school has blocked most social media sites, but not all the proxies, so it's easy enough to get around them. I look up Babs on everything, but I don't know their last name, and I find nothing.

I can't wait to know them.

The bell sounds and it's the start of recess, so I go to where I was sitting yesterday. The paperbark beside the patch of grass thrums with joy when it feels me, and I touch its trunk in greeting. It's slowly waking up from winter, shaking off the cold and getting ready to use its energy stores to bloom.

'Same,' I say to it out loud. I sit and unwrap my sandwich, and wait for Babs. I don't know if they'll want to sit with me again. There's a bubble brewing in my stomach, the nerves making me feel ill. I'm excited. I want them to sit with me.

I eat the jar of yoghurt and muesli Clover prepared for me this morning. She's given me some cheese and biscuits as well, tied up in a handkerchief-sized gingham cloth. Saltkin loves cheese; if he follows me to school I always share it with him. But he's busy today, it seems. The start of spring always means a lot of work.

Babs walks past with their jacket on. I can see patches on the sleeve. One has a green alien head and says, LET'S BE FRIENDS. The one under it is too small to read from where I'm sitting.

They turn their head, and they see me looking at them. 'I was looking for you.' They walk closer, and pause. I can see the uncertainty in their face, pausing, wanting to do something but ... too scared to?

'Same,' I say. And then I don't know what to say.

'Can I sit down?' they ask.

I move further back on the patch of grass under my tree and give them plenty of space. I always sit here, unless it's raining. Other grass is in the sun, or near too many people. This place is private enough, and there's no risk of sunburn.

'I know I asked already,' I say to Babs, 'but I literally have never seen you before.'

'I know, it's a thing about me. I feel like we should be friends.'

My eyes dart to the patch on their sleeve. 'Are you an alien?'

They laugh, and I'm glad they do. The patch under the alien says SHE/HER. As soon as I read it, something catches alight in me. She's made of fire, this girl. I think.

We don't say anything else the whole of recess, except when I offer her some cheese and she thanks me.

The rest of the day I don't see her, but the fire that she lit in me keeps me warm. At home, Saltkin meets me by the gate. He buzzes around my head, but because Moss and Clover must be nearby he doesn't speak. When we first met, I didn't realise not everyone could see him.

'Hey, sprout,' Moss says when I walk into the kitchen. This room is where everything seems to happen; it's the heart.

I kiss her cheek and sling my schoolbag onto the ground as I go to the cupboard to find something to eat.

'How was your day? Clover said you got up early.'

'It's spring, Moss.' I smile at her. 'I think I made a friend.'

'In spring?' She grins before taking a sip of coffee. 'I feel like you two go way back.'

'No, in a person. A girl at school.'

A lot of emotions go through her face while she pretends not to be relieved. It's not that I haven't had friends before, just they were all in primary school and the first couple years of high school. I kind of drifted from them, not really for any reasons. We didn't have anything in common.

The fire Babs has put in me is a thin flame, flickering a bit. It's not strong enough to stand near the tiniest of breezes yet, but I'm going to keep it safe.

Clover walks into the kitchen with a couple of branches of silver dollar eucalyptus. 'What?' she asks, looking at Moss's face.

'Iris made a friend,' she says.

'Have they?' Clover says brightly. 'Who? Do we know them?'

'Her name is Babs,' I say. 'We didn't really talk much, but I think she can tell.' She can tell that I am grown from a seed in the ground. I wonder if she knows I know she's made of fire. Probably. 'And I thought she was new. I've never seen her before, but she was on the bus this morning, and then in science.'

Clover laughs. 'Maybe magic is afoot.'

I do think she believes in magic, but maybe not to the same extent as me. The way she and Moss met definitely had some kind of magic going on, I'm sure, and I wasn't born the way other babies are. But I don't tell them about Saltkin, or his spell this morning. I want to keep it safe.

She starts to cut the branches so they'll fit into vases, enough to make the whole kitchen more alive. The kitchen and the garden are Clover's favourite places. She has plants strewn all through the house, but the kitchen gets the most love. The sun is just right, streaming through the windows at the best time of day. And we're always in here, and I know the plants like that. I can feel what they're feeling, sometimes, if I touch their leaves.

Saltkin tugs at my ear, wanting to talk.

'I should probably start my homework.'

'Well,' Moss says, 'keep us updated on the friend situation.'

'I will.'

I take my muesli bar to my room and close the door. After I turn on some dreamy electronic music, softly, I turn to Saltkin and say, 'I think it worked.' I take the rose quartz out of my pocket.

He claps his hands and a little peach cloud surrounds him. 'Oh!' he says, touching the stone with his tiny hands, his skin turning the same shade of pink. 'It worked.'

'Her name is Babs.'

'The fire girl,' he says. 'Oh yes. I know about her.'

'You know her?'

He nods. 'I haven't met her. But I know kinfolk who live nearby. She is very kind. She has been through too many things for someone so small. She's brave, Iris.'

A spark crackles through me, her fire. It's larger. 'Oh.'

He sighs contentedly, returning to his peach colours. 'How do you feel?'

'Like I'm on fire. In a nice way.'

He smiles as he sits on the windowsill, crossing his legs. 'Good. Just don't burn up.'

I hadn't considered that.

'Remember, you're made of plants.'

'I know, Saltkin.'

I close my eyes and feel the fire. It's warm, the flame still small, filling me up. I don't think she will burn me.

Chapter Two
The Fire Girl

As I'm staring out the bus window, I realise Iris won't see me again today. I take the rose quartz hanging around my neck and twist its coldness between my fingers. I try to ignore the sinking feeling as we get closer to their stop. I've seen them around school, and something about them always felt a bit magic. I realised yesterday while talking to them – they're made of plants. I don't know how that's true, but it must be like how I'm fire. Somehow it's real.

The bus pulls over, and a few people get on. I see Iris through the window. They're in our school uniform, shorts, itchy blue jumper.

They wave at me. I gasp.

When they're on the bus, they stop and hover. 'Can I sit next to you?'

'Of course!' I move my bag off the seat.

'I have the same,' Iris says as they pull a rose quartz out of their pocket.

I laugh in surprise, I can't help it. 'It's beautiful.'

Maybe they see faeries too, if they can see me. There's

something about the stone, maybe the way it shimmers, that makes me think so. In this town, anything could happen.

'I like your hair,' I say. It's cute, cut into a bob. They have a nice face, sharp cheekbones, soft eyes.

Iris screws up their face. 'Thanks. Your jacket is cute.'

Sometimes I feel like my jacket is armour. I put patches and badges on it, keep away people I don't want to talk to. When they can see me in the first place.

Though it's not part of our uniform I never get in trouble for wearing it at school, even when the teachers can see me. I'm not sure why.

I smile. 'Thanks.'

After we go to our separate homerooms, Iris is in science class. We've been in a few of the same classes for a couple of years, so I don't know why they can see me all of a sudden. And I don't know if they'll be able to see me again. As I sit next to them, I concentrate very hard on being opaque.

They smile at me. 'Hey again.'

'You use they pronouns, don't you?' I ask. 'I heard a teacher mention it.'

'I do. You're a she, right? Because of the patch on your jacket.'

I nod, warmth travelling up my limbs. Someone noticed.

The teacher clucks her tongue at us. 'Enough

chitchat, you two – you've got to get this done by the end of the lesson or we'll have to meet up at lunchtime.'

I smile to myself. It's not every day the teachers can see me, though I never get marked down as absent or missing a test. I've asked Mum about it, and though she didn't say it outright I think she's doing some spellwork behind the scenes.

Right now we're supposed to be learning about how liquid travels through barriers. Something about salt water and fresh water; they'll mix together if they're separated by a porous barrier. Which like, duh, but we still have to do the experiment. I get us both safety goggles from the tub even though all we're doing is pouring water into tubes.

'Thanks, Babs,' Iris says as I hand them the goggles. Hearing someone who isn't Mum say my name is so rare. I give them the biggest smile I can.

The water swirls as Iris pours it in, bubbles zigzagging to the surface. Tiny ones cling to the sides of the glass. I watch as they stir in salt, crystals dissolving slowly, the water turning cloudy at first.

'Do you want to come over?' I ask. 'Like, to my house. I have a movie I think you'd really like. My mum is making a lasagne tonight. It's a vegetarian one. Also, I have a dog.'

Their face warms up like the sun's shining on it. I realise then that they know I'm made of fire, burning, burning. Maybe that's why they can see me.

'I love veggies, especially in lasagne. And dogs! That sounds awesome.'

I smile so hard the safety goggles are pushed up my face. 'So you'll come?'

'I'll have to ask my mums, but it should be okay.'

I write down my number for them, trying not to let my hand shake. I hope their mums say yes. Even if they don't, hopefully Iris can see me on the bus anyway. And maybe at lunchtime.

In next period, maths, my phone buzzes in my pocket. The teacher doesn't look over, probably can't see me, so I get the phone out. It's Iris, and they're coming over! I grip my phone with both hands, bring it to my chest. I wonder if they're as lonely as I am – they must be. They're never sitting with anyone at lunch, or whispering to anyone in assemblies, or sitting next to anyone on the bus.

I leave class before the lunch bell. I go to where I saw Iris yesterday, the paperbark next to the patch of grass. As students start to come out of class, something in me sinks. I'm slipping, sliding through realities. It's like there are two worlds, and I know I'm totally in the second one right now. Iris won't be able to see me. I bite back tears. No. Just because they won't be able to see me now, they might later. It'll be fine. It'll be fine.

Iris comes out, sits down right next to me. They unwrap their sandwich and look around for me, face eager. I need to talk to them, so I call their phone – this connection, it can't break. Their eyebrows knit together as they feel their phone ring, frantically grabbing at their pockets till they find it. And when they see it's me, they relax a little, and look more confused than anything. 'Are you okay?'

'I'm okay,' I say, glad my voice isn't shaking. 'But I didn't want to text you this. I don't think you can see me anymore.'

'What?' Their face falls. 'I mean, we don't have to hang out, you can just tell me.'

'No! I mean, sorry, sorry, that was bad wording.' My heartbeat skips up. 'You know how you couldn't see me until yesterday, you thought I was new? I think I've slipped again.'

'Slipped?'

'Sometimes it happens. Should be okay by tonight, though.' I close my eyes and wish as hard as I can. *Please.* 'I'll see you on the bus?'

'Where are you?'

'Right next to you, Iris.' I hope it doesn't sound like I'm mad at them, they've done nothing wrong. 'Which is the problem, hey? But I'll see you on the bus. I'll try really hard. Okay?'

'Can I help?'

'Hm.' I've never had anyone outside of Mum and one of her witch friends know about me. 'I'm not sure. I'll think about it.' I hang up. Is there a way? It's not like I was born like this – the witch did this to me. I wonder what Iris thinks of all this. They must know faeries if they're this cool about it. Maybe they're even part-fae – there's *something* about them.

I take my lunch to the art room. Don't need the depressing hour of sitting next to Iris but not being able to talk, and art's my next class anyway. The room smells like oil pastels, paint, glue, imagination and spark.

Our art teacher, Miranda, comes into the room as the bell rings. Her eyes catch on where I'm sitting, but she doesn't acknowledge me. She starts to set up the tables, putting tubs of pencils and scissors on them, then stacks of paper. She sings something to herself in a language I don't understand.

Eventually Iris comes in and sits at the same table as me. They still don't see me, but the fire in me is stoked. They must know I'm here, on some level. I watch with wide eyes as a faerie appears on their shoulder. A little one, fat and peach-coloured. The two of them are chatting. I was right! The faerie sits on Iris's pencil case and watches them draw the shoes we're supposed to be copying. I never knew shoes were so hard to draw.

I hate shoes, I text Iris.

They giggle and I smile, watching them.

Miranda walks around, looking at everyone's work. She's always so kind, always finds something to be worthy of genuine praise. She pauses near me, but keeps walking past to Iris. She compliments Iris on the colour scheme of peach and green. The faerie, who is those colours, disappears into a glittery cloud of pink happiness.

I sigh. I can't just sit here and watch them, it's too weird. So I grab my things and walk out. No one calls after me.

After I get my bag from my locker, I wander the five minutes into town to my favourite cafe, Eaglefern. It has a couple of tables out front, and baskets of flowers hang off the awning. Inside, it's tiny and cute, filled with plants and natural light from the wall that is all windows. Tables are jammed into it, taking up every inch they can. It feels crowded, but in a cosy way. I love it here. There's art for sale on the walls – sparkling, whirling colours and glass and feelings. And the owner, Livia, can always see me.

The brass bell on the door trinks as I enter, and I slump onto a couch at the back of the cafe. Livia looks up from her newspaper. 'Babs, you're a bit early.' She always tries to get me to go to school properly, but she doesn't get it.

'Nah. Got any cakes that aren't selling?'

She rolls her eyes at me, but soon brings me a berry muffin. 'How's your mum?'

I shrug. 'Okay. The warmer weather helps.'

Livia sits on the couch opposite me. 'Can you give this

to her?' She presses something cold into my outstretched hand: a smooth, flat disc of tourmalinated quartz, the black rods of tourmaline suspended like they've stopped in time. Sometimes Mum does spellwork for Livia in exchange for money or useful objects.

'Where did you get this?'

'Oh, you know. Here and there.'

A customer walks in, and Livia leaves me on the couch holding this stone. I turn it under the lights, seeing the angles of the tourmaline, how everything sits suspended together. It warms my hand, and the warmth moves up my arm and into my heart.

It's windy as I walk to the bus. I rub the quartz between my thumb and palm. My stomach churns. *Come on*, I think to myself, *let Iris see me*. The quartz flares up. *Please*.

Iris is already on the bus, and as I get closer I realise they can't see me. I sigh but sit next to them anyway. The bus pulls away from the kerb, and someone's yelling at someone else for spraying their deodorant everywhere. Iris gets out a book and starts to read as people chat and throw things at each other. Iris sighs and stops reading, looking out the window instead. They send me a text: *You on the bus?*

And then I just pop up – I don't know how, but they turn and they see me. 'Babs!' They hug me, squeezing tight.

I hug back, and I can't stop smiling. The sparks in me are stoked, flying up. 'I think you know.'

'You're made of fire?'

I nod. Sometimes I crackle when I move and the flames flare out of me. 'And that I'm trans.'

'Me too.' Iris sighs. 'But I guess you know because of my pronouns. I don't look trans.'

I frown. 'You don't look not trans. You're trans, Iris, how else would you look?'

'I guess,' they say, but they're smiling. 'How much further do you live than me?'

'I'm only the next stop, and you could probably walk it, as long as you don't mind going through the forest. It doesn't have any paths to my house.'

'It has paths,' Iris says. 'Not everyone knows where they are, but they're there.'

'It makes sense that you'd know.' I pause, wonder if I should say the next bit. I know they're made of plants, energy stores and roots in dirt. 'Sprout.'

The rest of the bus trip we're silent. Iris starts to stand when their stop comes up, but then remembers at the last second. We stay on till my stop, surrounded by tree ferns, tiny pink flowers and moss.

'The walk's short,' I say as I grab my bag, 'though it's up a hill.'

I love our house. It's small but I love it. The outside is a creamy-pink, painted on weatherboards. Our garden looks overgrown but that's on purpose – it's chock-a-block with herbs, billy buttons, wildflowers and nasturtiums. The front door sticks when I open it, so I kick the bottom right corner and then we're in.

Me and Mum don't have a lot of furniture. But we've got big windows that look out into the garden. I take a deep breath. Mum's been cooking warm winter food. Sadie barks as she runs to the front door, her whole bum wagging with her tail. 'Hey, baby,' I say, smooshing her face between my hands. She sniffs Iris for a long, long time, and then licks their hand.

We got Sadie from a shelter. Everyone was wanting puppies, and she looked a little sad, tail wagging tentatively as I walked up to her. We're not sure what breeds she is, but she's just taller than my knees, with a big tail and a fluffy coat. She's got the friendliest face of any dog I've ever seen, which is how I fell in love with her.

'Mum!' I call out. We wriggle off our shoes, our socks wrinkly and off-white – only Year Sevens have nice socks.

'I'm in the bath, love,' Mum replies.

'Mum has a lot of pain,' I say to Iris as I lead her into the kitchen, Sadie following. 'She takes a lot of baths. Sometimes they're the only thing that helps.'

We have a vertical herb garden on the wall, and everything is in glass jars. We've got bunches of dried herbs in the window, and sun catchers ping glittering beads of light across the room. I can see Iris loves it.

I don't ask if they want something to drink, I just go straight for the banana and mango nectar and pour us glasses of syrupy-smooth goo. Iris downs half of it in one go, and I smile at them. 'It's my favourite.'

'It's so good! I have to save some of it. What's the movie you'd like to show me?'

'It's about rocket ships.' I grin. 'One's made out of a tree.'

'Huh.'

We set up in the lounge, Sadie lying across my feet, and I hand Iris some bikkies Mum made, still gooey in the middle. The chocolate is creamy, tingly on our tongues.

Our couch is old and squishy, and Iris sinks right in as they sit down. A few minutes into the movie, they have to pull themself up out of the cushions.

'Don't let it eat you,' I tell them. 'It'll do that.'

Iris laughs, but I'm serious. I give them a knowing look, then they seem to understand.

We finish the bikkies, licking goo off our fingers. My fire seems to be keeping us both warm. I don't really feel the cold much, which is why Sadie always tries to sleep on my bed in winter. I usually let her.

The spaceship that's made of a tree comes on screen, and Iris makes a noise. They lean forward, eyes hungry. I know the feeling, that this was made for you and no one else. The rest of the movie I barely hear them breathe. The credits roll and we sit in silence, and I can feel Iris digesting the movie, eyes closed.

After a while, they turn to me. 'How come I can't see you sometimes?'

'Well,' I say, my words sticky and chewy like I'm still eating the biscuits. 'It started when I was little. We were in the forest, me and my parents. I think we got lost. I don't know which one, or where it was. But anyway, I ended up on my own. I found a witch. She was more beautiful than any woman I've ever seen.'

I think she was the first trans woman I'd ever met, and she made it seem like anything was possible.

'And then we talked for a while, but I can't remember what about. It was when I was maybe … ten? Five or six years ago? I remember telling her I was made of fire, and she laughed and said it was obvious.'

Iris squeezes my hand.

'No one has been able to tell, I don't think, except you and Mum and the witch.'

'You're the only one who knows I'm born from a seed in the ground. Well, you and Clover and Moss. But what happened with the witch?'

'She confirmed I was made of fire … and then I can't remember. In my memory, feels like we talked for days. About everything. I know it's weird, but I think maybe something happened with time. Mum and Dad said I was only gone for five minutes. I remember sleeping, waking up in her house in the woods. She cooked awesome breakfasts. I made friends with the birds she'd feed.'

'She probably did manipulate time somehow, if you remember all that.'

'And then when I got back, I started to just disappear. Mum would stress, but she knew I would always come back. Dad ... he went strange. Not long after, he left us.'

'Strange?'

'I think maybe the witch revealed something, like our true selves? I don't know. I don't think he was ever a good person, Iris.'

'Do you miss him?'

'Sometimes. Not really. He doesn't even know I'm a girl.'

'I'm sorry he left.'

'For the best.' I smile tightly. I reach down to pat Sadie, and she huffs a big sigh. Sometimes I see dads with their kids and I don't miss *my* dad, I just wish I had a good one – one who would stay, and one I was glad had stayed.

'Babs?' Mum calls out. 'Dinner's ready.'

When we walk into the kitchen she's dishing up the lasagne, so I put Sadie outside. 'Need a hand, Mum?' I ask. 'I didn't hear you get out of the bath.'

'It's okay.' She smiles when she sees Iris. 'Hi, I'm Wendy.'

'Hello,' Iris says, quiet and shy.

Mum's a little shorter than me, and she always looks

so warm and tired and soft and strong. She's wearing a long floral dress.

'Thanks for coming over tonight,' I say.

We eat at the kitchen table after I grab a chair from my desk. The table is tiny and chipped and old, with words and symbols carved into it, but I don't think Iris really notices. There isn't a lot of elbow room, and Iris keeps bumping theirs into me. They say sorry every time, and I laugh and say it's okay. The kitchen fills with warmth.

'Babs tells me you met in science class,' Mum says.

'They first saw me on the bus.'

Iris nods. 'I'd never seen her before that day. But yes. And I saw the patch on your jacket, LET'S BE FRIENDS, so. I thought we should.'

'I told you something would come of it,' Mum says. 'She was hesitant buying the patch when we first saw it, and I just knew she had to have it.'

'Plus it looks cool.'

Mum laughs. 'Plus it looks cool.'

'This is really good, Mum,' I say, mouth full of lasagne. 'The best one yet.'

Iris nods in agreement as Mum beams. There's a lot to say, but we just eat. There's so much time ahead.

Mum finishes her dinner much faster than either of us, and then she says she has to go to bed. Me and Iris sit in the kitchen, not sure what to say to each other. We keep smiling and laughing, but not a lot of words come through the air between us.

And then I know one of Iris's mums is here, so I go open the door. Her hand is up, ready to knock. 'Oh, hello. Are you Babs? I'm Moss.'

'Hey, Moss.' I smile, then hand her a plastic container with some leftover lasagne. 'That's for you and Clover – Mum said we wouldn't eat the whole thing before it went off.'

'Oh.' Moss takes the container, surprised. 'Thank you.'

I want to ask her if she knows Iris is the most wonderful person in the world, and if they Iris shot up so they were as tall as Moss in one day, or did it take time? I want to know everything about them. But I don't ask, because there's plenty of time.

Chapter Three
The Smoky Quartz

Saltkin sits on my shoulder in the garden. I should be doing homework, but instead I'm sitting at the big wooden garden table that Moss built, staring at the moon roses. The sun is reaching them, and they shine luminescent under the rays. Sometimes I wonder if they're not petals, but instead are made of moonlight, or water, or satin. But always, when I get up close, I can see they're just plant, like me. I can see their veins.

Clover has planted a few different kinds of lavender. Some will have white flowers, some pink. Some will have two purple wings up the top. The bees love them, and so does Saltkin. When she was planting them he buzzed all about her, leaving sparkles in a trail.

Now he's walking around them with some of the other faeries, discussing the new lavender. I don't recognise all of his companions, but I know Elvie, Nidhogg and Eitri. They're a small crowd of bright colours, blending into the garden as they start to flitter about.

Elvie comes over and kisses my forehead before hovering in front of my face. She doesn't have wings; she's not as showy as Saltkin, but she's just as vain. 'Saltkin told me the spell worked. You still have the stone.'

'There are other stones, I know, but this one's my favourite. So I took it.'

'Good.' Her voice chirps like a tiny bird. 'He was so happy when you chose that one. It means love, you know.'

'Babs had one in the shape of a heart.'

'Extra.' She flutters up and down, blue sparks streaming behind her. 'That's good. Very good.'

'Just like the lavender.'

'And spring.' She closes her eyes for a second, relaxing in midair. 'There's more to come.'

'More of what?' I ask.

'More of anything.' She flits away, and I scowl.

Faeries don't lie, though I know they're able to twist the truth like I can hardly imagine trying to do. Sometimes they just won't tell me things.

I stand up, leave my homework on the table and walk over to Saltkin. He's still at the lavender, and I bend down to get to his level. 'What did Elvie mean?'

He pauses in his appraisal of the lavender. Clover's left the tags in the ground next to them, and this is the one that will bloom pink.

'I shouldn't tell you that. You'll find out.'

'Saltkii*iin*,' I whine, but he shakes his head.

'Something is happening in the forest. We can't spoil it for you, Iris.'

I nod. 'I suppose. How soon?'

'Soon enough.'

I leave him to the lavender and go back to my homework. It's for maths, and it's things we mostly covered last year. I skim through the problems, and they're easy enough. I like working with the shapes, I like that I can see how they make sense. I like graphs. Saltkin hates it; the other faeries didn't particularly like maths once I told them about it, but he hates it especially. He thinks these things don't need to be explained. I guess he doesn't realise that humans need maths to build bridges and homes; we can't eat flowers and live off sunlight.

I finish the problems, and I close the book. The tea I made earlier is cold by now, even though I only drank half the cup. I'm always bad at remembering to drink it. As I start to walk back into the kitchen a breeze picks up, and the eucalypts above rustle and chatter.

I feel like I have to go to the forest.

Saltkin with me, I step out onto the path beside the road. There is bush all around us, but to get to the walking tracks and the paths, the river, I have to go slightly further.

'Didn't you want to stay with the lavender?' I ask Saltkin.

He swoons a bit. 'I feel like today is a good day to be with you.'

'Is something bad going to happen?'

'*Something* is going to happen.'

'That's what Elvie said.' I sigh. Everything and nothing is real to him, I think. Or maybe nothing is true. I am still figuring it out.

We get to the start of the forest tracks, a car park. There are too many cars, too many people, chattering and thrumming away. It's the weekend, the first warm one in a while. Across the road, away from the main trails and the cafe, there is a smaller track. This one's nicer, and the river is there. No tourists seem to realise this, plus there's nowhere to have a picnic; it's all overgrown scrub.

We start to walk into the valley where the river lies. As we go down, it gets cooler – wet, misty. Saltkin drifts off the path, leaving a trail of peach-coloured sparks. He'll be back, or he won't be.

The forest is quiet. A bellbird's peal rings out, and there's the chatter of tinier birds. The wind runs through the leaves, sending whispered messages my way. They're too quiet for me to make out any meaning except that they're welcoming.

Sometimes the forest does not want people in it. I can tell, which means I'm safe. I worry about others, but nothing too bad ever happens out here. It's too overgrown for people to stray off paths, unless some kind of magic is involved. But they're safe today.

The ground under my shoes is soft, still cold from the winter months. The baby's tears and moss are still everywhere; they'll stay during spring, and summer, but they won't be as green or as spread out. I brush my fingers against some moss, and it knows me. It asks how I'm going. I haven't been out in a while. It doesn't use words, but the vague idea of them. I tell it about my loneliness, and about the moon roses. I tell it about Babs, and how she disappears sometimes. I tell it about the witch. It takes this all in, then I stand and move on.

Last night I decided the rose quartz should be on a necklace, and Saltkin wove me some rope. I'm not sure what it's made of, but I know it won't break. I want to tie it all together today, so I've got the quartz and the rope in my pocket.

I go down to the riverbank even though people aren't supposed to. There are signs saying how dangerous it is, that you could drown or get lost, that there are crumbling rocks, but the trees tell me where it is safe to stand. This whole area is safe, and I don't plan on swimming. I just reach down and dip my fingers in.

The river never knows who I am exactly. I can't talk to it and it moves too quickly to remember. If I came here more often, maybe it could; the tree by the bank, with the twisted trunk that loops right over the water, told me this last spring.

I drink from the river and I can taste the mountain.

Further along, just off the path, is a flat rock. There's enough room for a few people to sit down, and it's usually in the sun. It's my favourite place in the forest, and no one seems to go there, ever.

A crackly voice comes out of the trees. 'Sprout.' It's Vada, one of the dryads.

I turn and smile hello. Vada is a pine dryad, and their bark is cracked deep. When I met them, we talked a long time about how they weren't a girl. Dryads don't have the same gender system as humans. They had laughed for a long time before choking out, *Why on the mother's earth would we?* And then I asked if I could not be a girl too. They nodded. 'Dryads don't have a claim on this,' they told me. 'Hundreds of years ago, I met a person just like you. They didn't know, just like you. But dearest, you're like me.'

I've since learned there's an English word for this feeling, this strange and wonderful amorphous all-consuming wonder. Non-binary. It's not like this for everyone, and it's not like this for Vada, but they were the first contact I ever had with someone who didn't identify as a man or a boy, or a woman or a girl.

I asked Saltkin about this, and he confirmed that some faeries aren't men or women, but they are rare. And he has changed his gender many times over his life, and it doesn't seem to matter in the same way at all in faerie places. It's a quirk, like someone's hair colour. I tried to explain how it was ingrained into human life, in every respect, from birth, and I don't know if he believed me, or if he was capable of understanding how lost and trapped I felt before that day in the forest with Vada.

'Vada!' I stray off the path and go to them; they

embrace me, and we stay there, unmoving, just breathing in-out-in-out. There are blossoms in my rib cage.

'How have you been, my sprout?' they ask, once we are separate again. 'You have grown.' They place a hand on my heart. 'A lot, so quickly.'

'It's been so long, I'm sorry,' I say, realising that I haven't seen them since the summer. I breathe in the pine smell of them.

'I was away,' they say. 'I wandered far, I felt like I was lost. It's not often that dryads do.' They smile at me sadly. 'But we don't have our roots here.'

'Did it help?'

'Somewhat.' Still smiling, they put a hand on my shoulder. Vada told me how they were taken from their roots far away, brought here. But they don't know how to get back, so they wander here. Just watching everything, not interfering.

I hug them again. Their body is never hard exactly, but never as soft as flesh.

'I found someone like me,' I say. They're leading me deeper into the forest, and I follow them without hesitation. I don't know where we're going, and I could never get back on my own, but they have never done me any wrong.

'A human? Plenty of you around.' They look over their shoulder and grin at me.

'Ha-ha.' I pause to step over a tree trunk that's fallen across the path. It's covered in slippery moss, and I take extra care not to slide. 'She's trans too. A girl, so we're not really the same. But she understands.'

'From your school?'

'Yes. She lives near here. Her mum cooked us lasagne yesterday. I think she's a witch.'

'Her, or her mother?'

'Her mother. Well, maybe both.'

'Sprout, that's so wonderful.'

'She's made of fire.'

'Be careful,' they warn me. 'Fire burns, and when it catches, it can go quickly.'

'Saltkin said the same thing. I'll be careful.' Vada is made of wood, so I guess it's a sensitive topic for them. 'How long were you in the snow?'

'All through the winter. I got back today, and I wanted to see you. I'm glad you got my message.'

I remember the chattering eucalypts above my house.

Vada says, 'I have something for you.' Then they fall silent again.

I'm curious, but I decide to let them tell me in their own time.

We get to a huge tree, so wide I could never put my arms fully around it. Sometimes, I wish I could be sucked into the trunk and be absorbed until all I would think about is the sunlight on my leaves, so high above the ground. When I hug it my arms stretch out either side of me, I can barely feel the curve.

The tree welcomes me, breathes in my breath.

'Here,' Vada says, pointing to the base where there's a tiny cave, sheltered from the rain and the wind and the general violence that exists in the world.

'What is it?' I ask, reaching down. There's something cold inside. I draw my hand out, and it's a crystal point. I think it's also a quartz, smoky-clear.

'From the snow mountain,' they say. 'It will be best if you pick it up yourself.'

I clutch it to my chest. 'Thanks, Vada.'

'Any time,' they say, smoothing hair from my face. 'I'll take you to your rock now.'

The forest is denser than usual, but Vada convinces the plants to move out of the way just a smidge. We get near to the human path, and the rock is just around the corner. Vada stops right before we reach the path; they hug me goodbye, squeezing my arm before letting go. 'Good travels, my sprout.'

'I'm glad you're back,' I say, and they return to the forest, melting into the trees and the ferns, the spiky bushes down near my shins.

The rock is in the full sun. When I sit down, it's warm against my bum and legs; I pause, close my eyes, let the light warm my face. The smoky quartz makes a little clunk as I set it on the ground in front of me, and I get out the rose quartz and the rope Saltkin made. I start tying knots over the quartz, making a net to keep it safe as it hangs around my neck. Saltkin made the rope long enough so that I can pull it over my head and keep the stone under my shirt. I wonder if he created it with magic, his hands, or both.

I slip on the necklace, put the smoky quartz safe in my pocket and lie on the rock. Its warmth radiates into my back, and the sunrays are on my front. I feel like I'm floating in soft fire. The rays are filtered by the gumleaves, so they're not burning hot.

Saltkin returns, chattering away in another language that he's forgotten I don't speak. Or maybe he just doesn't need me to understand. His bird-light bones mean I can barely feel him as he walks across my torso. Sometimes he flits up into the air and will appear on the other side of my chest.

'You know I don't know what you're saying?' I tell him.

'I'm talking to the magpie,' he says.

I peek an eye open and see the bird sitting on a tree nearby. Its head is cocked. I wonder if it's going to try and eat him. That happens sometimes.

I say, 'I love their warbles.'

'I'll pass on the message.'

I close my eyes again as Saltkin keeps chittering away, his pitch up and down, warbling. He stops, the magpie sings something, then there's silence. Saltkin lies down on my chest, right next to the rose quartz, and we doze off in the softened fire of the sun.

Chapter Four
The Other Realm

The trees are soft today as they sway in the breeze. No school, I've got better things to do. This morning when I told Mum I wasn't going, she asked if I could get her some flowers in the other realm. Sadie wants to come with me, but I'm not sure how dogs go there, so I told her to stay at home.

I walk out of our backyard into official national park territory. Technically I'm not allowed to be in this spot, I'm supposed to stick to the tracks, but no one's ever around to tell me not to. And I'm always careful not to snap a branch or step on a seedling.

Now I have to get to the other realm. Sometimes it's easy, but sometimes it just doesn't want me there. Slippery, I guess, a bit like me. Maybe that's why I find it easier than Mum.

I keep walking, making sure I don't step on any plants that aren't supposed to be stepped on. Sometimes I watch people on the trails crushing ferns and flowers. I tell them off, but they never listen to me, really. Just think I'm a weirdo.

I focus on my feet – the rhythm's important. Focus on not-being present. I feel the squeeze, the change in the air. My ears pop, and I think I'm there. Sometimes it's hard to tell, because lots of things look the same. When a purple bumblebee flies past, I know I'm in the right space. They don't exist on mainland Australia, they're from where the dryads and the faeries are from. Just like Mum's flowers. She uses them in some of her spells. The petals stay purple for a really long time, longer than lavender, so they're good ones to use as a replacement sometimes. They've got most of the same properties, but she likes the smell better.

I get a nerve-electric zap up my arm. Nova's close by. I wish they'd just use a phone or something to let me know, instead of zapping me all the damn time. 'Nova?' I hear the slow creak of wood moving. I scowl – I'm not going to look for them, they can come to me.

The ferns and trees seem to part as I get closer to the meadow. It always takes a different amount of time to get here, and one time I swear I was walking for a full day. The sun's in front of me and shines through the flower petals: red, purple, yellow, orange. Leaves light up too, and the fuzzy stalks of the poppies. Birds and crickets are singing, and a few bees are flying between flowers.

Way better than school.

I take off my backpack and leave it at the edge of the meadow. Then I walk through the long stalks of flowers, the grasses itching my legs a little as I brush past. Some of the flowers are the ones that we find in the regular world, like daisies and native flowers, but others are ones that only grow in the realm – ones that sparkle in the daytime. The ones Mum wants can be hard to find, sometimes the buds hide under their own leaves like secrets waiting to be unravelled.

When I crouch down, the crickets stop singing around me. I peer through a few stems and find the first bud. I pick it gently, then put it in the jar in my pocket. It takes a while, and I get a few thorns in my skin, but soon the jar is half-full.

'Babs,' an old voice says, like wind rustling through reeds.

When I stand and turn around, I see Nova. A birch dryad, they are tall and spindly. Some small marks on their bark, where branches have fallen or been torn off, look like eyes. The eyes are all over their body. Sometimes I swear I see them move.

'What are you doing here?' they say in their breeze-like way. 'The realm isn't safe for you.'

'You've told me that one hundred times, Nova. It's fine. I got it.' I try not to roll my eyes, but I can't help it. I screw the lid on the jar and put it back in my pocket.

'This is different.'

'Why?'

'Something is happening.'

41

The hairs on my body rise up. 'Be specific.' Nova seems serious, which worries me. I try to focus instead on finding flowers for Mum.

They sway in the breeze, closing the eyes on their face. 'There is something in the air.'

'Cool.' I bend down and keep looking for buds.

'Babs, you should listen to me.'

'Nova, no offence, but you tell me stuff all the time about how I'm going to get hurt, or something's dangerous, or the air is trying to kill me, or whatever else, and like, I think I'll be fine.'

Their trunk creaks as they sigh. 'I do wish you would listen to me, I –'

'I know, I know, you're very wise.' I find three buds and pluck them, putting them into the jar. 'Oh, by the way, Mum made you something.' Before they can respond, I get up and get to my backpack. I pull out a little globe filled with herbs and rocks. 'It's for protection,' I say, handing it over. It sparkles in the sunlight, sending out a tiny rainbow for a split second.

They make a pleased hum, then loop the string over one of their branches. 'Tell her thank you, and I miss her company.'

I nod. 'You should come into the backyard again sometime, she'd love to see you.'

Nova nods back. 'I will.'

The breeze picks up, smelling of a memory I can't place. Just faintly, and then it's gone.

'Do you really think I shouldn't be here today?'

'I would not lie to you.'

'Can you take me to Iris?'

I don't know if Nova knows who Iris is exactly, but I do know I can feel them somewhere in the forest, back in the regular world. I just hope they can see me. Whenever we part, I worry. What if it's the last time?

As Nova guides me to the path, the wind picks up around them, making them sigh and creak with every movement.

'Thanks,' I say when we're at the right spot. 'I'll tell Mum to come see you soon.'

Nova just wheezes out some wind. Then they're gone.

I sit on a log that's fallen. After a few minutes, Iris appears in maroon shorts and a t-shirt with flowers all over it. Their face lights up when they see me. 'Hey,' I say, like we had planned all this, 'what took you so long?'

'You took school off too?'

I shrug. 'Yeah, y'know. Sometimes you just gotta. Anyway, I want to show you something. Follow me.' I jump off the log and start down the path, looking over my shoulder to make sure they're following me.

'Is it far?'

'Sometimes.'

We stray off the path into the forest, crossing the river at a narrow point. There are heaps more birds here and their songs are louder, freer, they bounce off each other and we're surrounded by their music. We get to a tiny dirt path that weaves through the trees. This leads to the side of a dirt road, and the path continues on the other side of it. Eventually, it's finally wide enough for us to walk side by side.

'Nice stone,' I say when I notice they're holding a smoky quartz in their hand.

'Thanks.' They lift it up, catching the sides in the light. 'I found it in the forest.'

'Huh. That's pretty cool.'

They pass it to me and it's warm from their hand. 'Yeah, I couldn't really believe it. Do you reckon they really send out those vibrations people say they do?'

'Not sure.' I give Iris back their stone. 'Sometimes I think maybe they do, and sometimes I reckon I'm just imagining it. But either way, they're pretty and fun.'

'I was looking up the rose quartz that Salt— that I have, and it's supposed to mean love. I don't think, like, that's a real thing written into the chemical makeup of the stone, but because whenever I think about the stone I think about that meaning. And I guess like, I don't know, it kind of makes it real.' They blush.

'That makes sense. And there's not like, it's not dangerous to think this stuff? It's not hurting anyone.'

'And it's fun.' Iris sighs in relief.

I laugh. 'And it's fun.'

The road we're on turns from dirt to bitumen, and

soon we're at the main street of town. We walk past the newsagents, op shop, a few cafes, bakeries, then we come to Eaglefern.

I say, 'This is my favourite cafe.'

'I've never been here before,' Iris says. I can tell they like the plants. 'Moss and Clover say we have to keep money for other things.'

'Livia gives me free stuff sometimes, she's friends with my mum. Come on, I'll show you.' The bell dings as we walk in.

There's no one sitting in here, and when Livia sees me, her face lights up. 'Hi, girls.'

Iris grips my hand. The bottom of my stomach falls out. I want Iris to feel safe in this cafe, just like I do. It smells like my kitchen.

I look at Iris, eyebrows raised. Iris nods. I shake my head. 'Livia, Iris isn't a girl.'

Livia puts down her tea towel. 'Sorry. Is he your boyfriend?'

I scowl. 'First of all, why would I want to date a boy? And Iris is non-binary.'

'Sorry, love, I don't know what that means.'

'It means,' Iris says, voice cracking a little. I grip their hand tighter and they continue, 'It basically means that I'm not a boy or a girl.'

'Oh.' Livia chuckles. 'I didn't know that was allowed.'

'Livia!' I shriek. 'That's so rude!'

'Sorry. Sorry. I've never met anyone like you, Iris.'

'It's not a joke!' I didn't know my voice could get so high.

'Look, I'll make it up to you, sweetheart. Free coffees today, and a cake each. I'll teach myself and then next time you come in, if I'm rude, well, we'll work out something.'

I glance at Iris. They nod, a little sadly, and I wish I could take it all back. Iris does change their order to a hot chocolate, though, and I do the same. We sit at a couch next to the window, with flowerboxes right outside, filled with every colour flower. Fat blue-striped bees are hovering over them.

I tell Iris, 'I come here almost every day no one can see me. Livia always can.'

'Is she a witch?' Iris asks, quietly, like they don't know if that's a rude thing to say.

I shrug. 'I think so.'

'Are you, Babs?'

I shrug again. 'Dunno. I guess.'

'Can you become a witch? Do you have to be a girl?'

As Iris says this, Livia comes over with our drinks. 'You're already one, if you want to be,' she says. 'You can talk to plants.'

Iris blushes deeply, not sure what to say.

'I'm sorry I called you a girl,' she says. 'I didn't know there was anything else.'

'I didn't either, at first,' Iris says.

'I'll leave you two to it, then.' Livia wanders back up to

the front. The place is just big enough that we can have a conversation without really being overheard by Livia, although we have to keep our voices down.

'My mum's a witch,' I tell Iris. 'Hey, let's do like a spell or something later. Instead of homework. It's more fun.'

'That sounds good.'

I sip my hot chocolate. It's warm fizzy good, like the cookies Mum makes. Something about witches and chocolate makes it taste better. 'Mum does spells for money.' I lean forward a bit, speak lower – I've never told anyone this. I've not had anyone to tell. 'She can't have a regular-person job because of the fibro, but she can do this.'

'Fibro?'

'Fibromyalgia. It's … complicated. Basically, it's a chronic thing. She's in a lot of pain, pretty constantly.'

'Do the baths and stuff help?'

'Only, like, for comfort. Like they're more for her depression, I think, than anything.' I breathe out deep, sit back into the couch and close my eyes. 'I don't think I've said that out loud before. She has a hard time. Anyway.' I smile and have some more hot chocolate. 'She could probably lend you some books. If you wanted to learn. About magic.'

'That could be fun.'

We watch the bees outside the window. They love the sage especially, and the little white-and-purple daisies.

'Come over tonight?' I ask. 'Stay if you want. Mum will show you some things.'

'I dunno if I'm ready yet,' Iris says. 'For the spells, I mean. I'd like to stay.'

Chapter Five
The Haircut Spell

When we're at Babs's, her mum is asleep anyway. Her bedroom door is shut, and some kind of power is radiating out from it, though I don't know now if it's my imagination because Babs told me she is a witch, or if it's from something else.

Babs shows me her mum's library of magic books. 'She's got heaps of stuff. If you ever want to borrow something, you can ask her.'

'Wow.' I look at all the titles. There are books about the moon, dreams and palmistry, and lots about herbs and cooking. There are some books on crystals, too.

We make dinner out of a few leftovers in the fridge, watch another movie, and end up doing our homework. I'm in the higher maths class than Babs, so I help her out.

'Babs ... do you think a haircut would count as a spell?'

Babs takes my hair, not a handful, not a tiny bit. Somewhere in between. Her breath is warm on my skin, rushing past the hairs on my neck, sweeping over my shoulder blades.

'How much?' she asks. Her voice is closer than it has ever been, somehow. Closer than when she leans into my ear to whisper something in class, closer than when we're hugging and say goodbye. These words are so close they heat every part of me in a way I don't understand, and it scares me a little.

'All of it.'

Like a plant, it'll grow back stronger, bushier, quicker, if you cut it at the right time.

I don't know if I want it to grow back.

She takes another curl in her hand, lets it fall through her fingers like water, like sand. 'Are we talking a pixie cut or stubble?'

'Stubble.'

I need it gone, and right now she's the only one who can give me what I want. She'll do it right, I know.

'I'm going to cut it off so it's short and then shave it, is that okay?'

I swallow, and I want to stop, to take it all back. I can keep the length and I can keep hating it. Nothing needs to change. But I say, 'That's okay.'

She keeps her hands on my hair for just a moment, and then she lets me go. A pang of loss in my ribcage blossoms into something else when she touches me again, sparks flying up to my throat. 'Okay,' she says, breathy. 'Let's go.'

She begins at the bottom of my head where it starts to become my neck. The scissors are so close to my skin, there's a scrape against my head a couple of times, but she never hurts me. When she's near my ear, she cups the soft skin to make sure she doesn't cut anything by accident. In the mirror, her brow is furrowed in concentration. She's not looking at me, and I think if she did right now, well, I don't know what I would feel. She is taking parts of my body away; I asked her to. It's strange when I think of it that way.

Half my hair is gone; I'm lopsided, I'm uneven. It feels right, I feel more of myself. My eyes fill with tears.

'You okay?' she asks.

A tear slips out, barely brushing my cheek before it falls onto my arm. 'Yeah,' I say. She grips my shoulder and I put my hand on hers, just holding. She's got bits of my hair on her fingers and they get everywhere, some falling onto my arm where the tear fell. There is no going back. 'Please keep going.'

'You sure?'

'All or nothing, right?'

It's like some part of me is dying. There's loss, but something new's going to emerge. Tiny bright-green shoots.

She smiles at me in the mirror. 'Right.'

I let her hand go and she continues, maybe a bit slower.

All the length is gone soon, an age later – it's been minutes but it's been years. The centimetres left behind are uneven and ugly, short and long, and I love them.

She turns on the clippers and brings them closer; I can feel the vibrations in my bones.

'Wait,' I say as I turn to face her, properly face her.

She turns off the clippers but otherwise doesn't move.

'I want to keep it like this. I love it.'

She smiles again and puts down the clippers. 'You look great.'

I want to be seen. I want to be recognised. I feel like she's given me that.

'Want a shower?' she asks. 'I can give you a fresh shirt that's not covered in hair.'

'Yes, please.'

She gives me a shirt that says THIS MUST BE MY DREAM, a towel, a face washer. She shows me how to work her shower and then leaves me alone in the bathroom, standing in the warmth of the light. It's an old room; some of the wood has rotted away near the base of the shower from time and too much water. Ours is the same.

When I undress, my hair that was caught in my clothes falls to the floor. Pieces of me not mine anymore.

The water cleans me, warms me. When I dry myself off I sweep up the slivers of hair with my hands and put them into the bin with the toilet rolls and the tissues and the cotton balls. All waste, now. I step into her clothes and they're soft, slightly bigger than my own.

My hair's now a little jagged, strange, but it shows off the bones in my face. Without the frame of soft curls, my features look squarer. More like myself.

Babs is sitting on her bed, reading. 'Did you want to stay up for a bit?'

'Not really. But you keep reading, it's okay.'

She swivels around and gets under the sheets; I curl up beside her, my head resting on her hip. She reads out loud now, without me asking, tales of trees and magical lands, and I fall asleep as she moves her hand across my new hair, her fingers gentle and warm.

Chapter Six
The Rose Boy

On Monday there's a new boy in science class. He's tall and gangly, thick black hair just past his chin, light-brown skin. When the teacher introduces him, I know from how he shies away from her that it's not his real name. He takes a seat in the front row by himself.

His books and uniform are all new. The shirt still has creases from where it was folded in the packet. When he leans forward a bit, I see he's got shaved sides.

I look at Iris and know they're thinking the same thing: this boy, he's like us. I trace a sigil on my thigh and concentrate on the air around him to see if it reveals anything, but he's mysterious, not giving anything away.

Throughout the lesson I hope we'll split up into groups so I can go talk to this boy, but we're on a new topic – rocks and rock formations. We're just reading and answering questions in the textbook.

Maybe if I had any control over this curse, I could disappear from everyone else except him, and we could have a chat. Maybe I could even extend this to him. He looks like he needs someone to talk to. He looks lonely.

The boy stays hunched over his books the whole lesson. His sleeves are too long for him and he holds the ends in his palms. As soon as the bell rings, he packs up everything, quick as, and leaves without looking at anyone. Before we met, Iris would do this. Just leave.

There's a twinge in my guts as I walk down the hall. 'Hey, can you hear me?' I ask Iris when the twinge happens again. They don't respond. I think of just going home, but then I wonder if maybe the new mysterious boy is in my next class, or maybe we could find him at lunch. Maths is next, though, and I don't want to go.

I trace a sigil on my forearm for clarity and decide instead to go to the library. The twinging seems to have stopped – I reckon I might be visible again, but I really don't want to go to maths. On the way, I see the new boy. He's taken off his jumper, and on the back of his arm, just under his shirtsleeve, a small rose is pinpricked into his skin.

'Hi,' I say.

He startles and whips around, all long limbs and floppy hair. 'Hello,' he says, clutching his books to his chest.

'I'm Babs.'

He tells me the name the teacher said, but it doesn't match his face at all. It drops out of his mouth like a pebble to the bottom of a river.

'That's not your real name, is it.'

He stares at me. 'How did you know?'

I shrug. 'Magic,' I say and smile. 'I use she pronouns, by the way.'

'Babs,' he says, rolling my name like a lolly in his mouth. 'I'm not sure what I want my name to be.'

'You don't need to, not right now. I can just call you boy, if you want.'

'I mean, I would like to.'

'I can help you. And Iris too – they're non-binary. They're really sweet.'

'Thanks.' There's a pause, and we look everywhere but each other. 'Um, I'm supposed to get to the B building, where is that?'

I take him up a flight of stairs and down a few hallways. We pass people in classes, but no one bothers to check why we're just wandering. 'If you want to sit with us at lunch, we'll be near the gym. Under the paperbark. Iris has really short hair, usually sits cross-legged. Will probably have a cheese sandwich.' I don't tell him I might be invisible – I guess he'll find out soon enough, and he should be okay as long as he can sit with Iris. 'Oh, we're in the same maths class,' I realise when we get to the door he needs. 'The teacher's really cool, I reckon you'll have a good time. She won't care that you're late.'

'You're not coming?'

I shake my head. 'I've got … something else.'

He frowns a little but doesn't bug me about it. I wave goodbye as he goes into the classroom, and he sits alone up the front. I watch him for a sec as the teacher talks to him. He nods and smiles politely. I could go hang out in Eaglefern, but maybe I shouldn't leave him alone. He was all alone in science, too. I sigh, then open the door. No one notices me walk in, and the teacher doesn't notice as I sit down. The boy looks around. 'Are you invisible?' he asks as he leans towards me.

I nod. 'Sometimes. It's hard to explain. I was cursed by a witch.'

'Huh.' He takes it in. 'My dad did say we'd have an interesting time here.'

'It's an interesting town.'

'Does the witch who cursed you live here?'

'Some do. Not this one. I can't find her, though sometimes I try.'

'To lift the curse?'

I nod.

'How come the teacher doesn't notice when I'm talking to you?'

'Not sure. The curse seems to like, cover people I'm in contact with. And it's like, I'm never marked as absent from class. And even if they can't see me during a test, they'll take my finished paper when I offer it to them. I don't get it.'

The teacher asks us to do problems from the textbook. I don't really understand graphs much. I can do anything else. But graphs confuse me. And I never have anyone to ask, really. Iris is in a different maths class, not learning this stuff.

I watch the boy as he gets out his ruler and starts to draw the axes. 'How do you do that?' I ask, and he shows me with steady hands how to figure out where the dots go, how to connect them with a line. I still don't quite understand by the end of class, but then the bell rings for lunch and I disappear from him. 'Boy?' I ask, and I can see his confusion, the way he looks right through me. The way he can't see my pencil case or books on the table anymore. 'I'm still here,' I say, though I know he can't hear me. 'You should go sit with Iris. They're lovely. They'll love you.'

He packs up his things and with a last look at where I was sitting, he heads out the door. I sit in the classroom till it's empty.

I bring my arms up onto the desk and rest my forehead on them. I wish the witch had never found me, I wish I could be seen all the time. I close my eyes and try to concentrate on being solid, being seen. But I know it doesn't work, somehow. I feel like a fog, like fairy floss, like I'm not quite real. A shadow, made of static.

I breathe in as much as I can, exhale all at once. *Get up, Babs.* When I try the door, it's locked. 'Come on!' I yell, twisting the doorknob, but it won't budge. It hasn't not even got a little snib that I can turn to unlock it, which seems hugely unsafe.

I roll my eyes and think through all the spells I know. Any for unlocking? Mum's probably taught me heaps. But then she says the most important part is intention.

I press my hand to the door and focus really hard, trying to imagine it unlocked, me walking through it.

I try the handle again. Damn.

The window's open a tiny crack, though, and there's a big branchy tree outside. It takes a bit to push the window, an old heavy thing, open all the way. There's a staircase underneath, concrete and bricks. If I fall, it's not going to be soft.

I go back to grab my books and pencil case, then drop them out the window. They splay out over the ground. I take a deep breath and grab the closest branch, tugging on it gently to make sure it can bear my weight.

With both hands, I grip. Tight, release, tight, release. *I can do this.*

I let myself drop off the windowsill. My arms protest as I shimmy down the branch until my feet can reach the bigger one underneath, closer to the ground. The tree groans.

'Oh!' I stop moving.

The tree brings a few branches closer to me, and at first it looks like it's going to flick me off like an unwanted fly. But the branches pause, and I reach out, and then they form steps to help me get down.

When my feet hit the concrete, I realise I'm shaking. 'Thank you,' I say, touching the trunk. That would have taken a lot of energy. A couple of leaves fall off the branches.

I sit with the tree for the rest of lunch, breathing next

to it, hoping to transfer some of my energy back. I trace sigils on its trunk.

I jerk awake to the bell. Scrambling to pick up my things, I say goodbye to the tree and run off to art. It's always the hardest to stay visible in this class, but hopefully I'll get to see Iris.

I take a seat next to them and they hug me.

'Sometimes I still can't believe you can see me,' I say as we get out our sketchpads. 'I'm so scared you'll stop altogether one day and I'll be alone again.' I pull out a red pencil and start to draw little squiggles, a network of them, feeding into each other.

'We can still talk through the phone,' they say.

'Did a boy come and sit with you at lunch, by the way?'

Iris raises their eyebrows. 'No? What boy?'

'The new one from science. I said he could sit with us, but then I disappeared. Oh –' I wave at the boy as he enters the room. 'You're in the same class! Sit with us.'

He sits opposite me and Iris, runs a hand through his hair. 'Hey.'

'This is Iris. And Iris, this is the boy. He doesn't have a name yet.'

Miranda starts talking so we don't say anything else, but Iris sneaks a couple of glances at him. I think they've picked up, like I have, that he's not sure what he's made of. I'm fire, they're plants, but he doesn't know. He's new, like a bright dawn.

We're supposed to start using whatever material we want to create something that describes our last birthday party, which I don't really see the point of. The thing about art class, I guess, is that I don't really see the point in general. This is the lead-up to our big project at the end of term, exploring ourselves and our feelings. Whenever Miranda mentions it, tiny sparks flicker and grow in my stomach.

The boy is staring at his brand-new sketchpad – he looks lost. I want to tie a rope to his leg because I feel like he might float away. 'Are you okay?'

He has a new tin of the pencils we're supposed to buy for school next to him. The plastic is still on them. I've got a bunch of pencils from the two-dollar shop, held together by an old hair tie.

'I, uh, my last birthday party was –'

'For someone who wasn't exactly you?' I ask.

He nods. 'Kinda, yeah.'

'I don't think I've ever had a birthday party,' Iris says. 'Except for when I was a baby. But then I guess that was more for my parents, instead of me.'

I laugh. 'My last birthday was when I was still trying to convince myself I was a boy.'

'I think we could just imagine what our like, ideal birthday party would be. And draw those. Otherwise we're just gonna be sad.'

'That does sound like more fun,' the boy says. With a fingernail he slices open the plastic covering his pencils, then he picks up the green. He draws an oval and starts filling it in.

I tap my pencil against the table. 'I don't know what mine would be.'

'Do you have a favourite cake? Or like, kind of dessert?' Iris asks.

I shrug. 'I guess like, just butter cake. It's so nice. Or maybe ...'

'What?'

'Oh, I really love lemon meringue. But it's so expensive.'

'Clover, one of my mums, can make a really nice lemon meringue,' says Iris. 'It's Moss's – my other mum's – favourite, so their recipe is perfect. Just say, at this party, I'd gift you a lemon meringue.'

I beam at Iris. 'That's really cute.'

The boy's page is full of green balloons.

Chapter Seven
The Faerie Bond

The bell that means the end of school sounds and I grab my things, heading to my locker right before the rush of everyone else trying to get their bags out first. It's so busy and crowded that I don't wait for Babs and just start walking down the hill, away from school, then up the main road.

The op shop has a boxload of free books out the front, so I take a look. I can hear something humming, and so I keep digging through the books. There's a lot of science fiction and romance. The humming seems to be coming from deeper than the box goes, and I keep sticking my hand in further and further.

I gasp as a shock of static electricity runs up my arm. By now, I'm more than elbow deep into a box that looks like it's only maybe twenty centimetres tall. My hand grasps the cover of a book; it feels clothbound and like it's falling to pieces, and I pull it up through everything else. Its cover is faded, and the gold lettering says something in another language. There is a toadstool on the front. The binding is definitely coming apart, and the pages are all mottled with water damage on the sides. It doesn't stop humming in my hands.

I stuff the book into my bag and get to Eaglefern. I sit down before ordering, then bring out the old book and lay it on the table. I carefully open it; the first few pages are blank. I keep flicking through. They're all blank. It smells like old book, it looks worn and loved, so why isn't there anything in it? I frown, close the book again. It must've been humming for a reason.

I shove it back into my bag when I hear Livia coming towards the table. She brings over a hot chocolate, says it's for free again. 'I read up,' she adds. 'I didn't realise it was so important. I like your new hair.'

'Now you know,' I say. 'Thanks.' There aren't any hard feelings here, and I'm glad I didn't just write it off. I think sometimes it's important to, but Babs knows this woman, and respects her, so trying wasn't wasted.

With Clover and Moss, it was easy: they both understood straight away. I didn't even have to explain, it just clicked. Maybe because I was a plant baby.

The hot chocolate is fizzy good, as Babs would say, warming me up right to the ends of my fingers.

When Babs arrives, she's soaked; it's started to rain. She grins at me, though, and we sit and drink before heading to the bus. When we get to her place, our uniforms are dripping because neither of us thought to take an umbrella. Wendy brings us some towels, and then when we're dry enough we go to Babs's room to get some dry clothes.

She lets me have the first shower. When I step in, that burst of warm water feels better than anything else. I close my eyes and put my head under the stream. The water rushes past and warms me right to my shivering bones. I get out before I use up all the hot water, then dry myself off with the towel Wendy gave me. It's fluffy like one from a hotel in a movie, and warm from sitting under the heating light.

I feel new, fresh, like those two first leaves I was when I poked through the soil.

I pull on the clothes Babs lent me, then I leave the bathroom and she has her shower. I sit in the kitchen, and her mum has just put on the kettle. 'Would you like a tea?' Wendy asks, getting out a second cup for me.

'Please.'

She fills the pot with steaming water and brings everything over to the table. 'I'm glad Babs met you,' she says after she sits down. 'She's never really been able to keep friends, because of how she disappears.'

'I can imagine. I'm glad she told me, otherwise I guess I would have thought she'd kept flaking out on me. And it's nice that she trusted me enough.'

'She could tell you were a good person,' Wendy says. She rotates the teapot three times clockwise before pouring out the tea. She pushes the milk jug towards me and opens the honey jar. 'We've got sugar as well, if you prefer. But this honey is from our own bees.'

'What? Babs didn't tell me you had bees!'

I'm actually more surprised that Saltkin didn't tell me; he loves bees.

'I don't know if I can teach you magic,' she says unprompted, so I guess Babs must've told her. 'The way I learned was by feeling my way through everything. There's no one right way to be magical. I'm not sure if anything that works for me will work for you.'

'How did you learn?'

'When I was a teenager, I was in the hospital a lot. I read a lot of books – this was before the internet. There was only daytime telly, which wasn't great. One day another patient was released, and they left behind a book. It was about magic, about plants and what they can mean. I love working with herbs. I feel as though you'll like crystals.' She nods to the rose quartz dangling around my neck. 'That's a pretty rope you've got.'

I wonder if I should tell her that Saltkin made it. Although I feel like she knows.

'Maybe if you help me make dinner,' she says, 'that's a good place to start.'

'What's for dinner?'

'Not sure. Something with lentils.' She opens a cupboard and takes me through all the ingredients, deciding that she's going to make a vegetarian bolognese.

'I'm not a vegetarian exactly,' she says, cutting up some vegetables, 'but I try to eat less meat. We really only have it when we go out. Which isn't a lot.'

I hear Babs's shower stop, and some clattering around in the bathroom.

'She likes to take her time,' Wendy says. 'Sometimes she'll be in there for hours. Which is only a slight exaggeration.' Wendy's laugh is like a waterfall, just like Babs. 'Can you fill the pot with water so it covers these by a couple centimetres?' she says, putting the vegetables and lentils in the pot.

I lug it over to the sink and do as she says, then place it on the stovetop.

'Now, the fun part.'

On the wall, a vertical herb garden has been grown in jars. She plucks some leaves from a couple of plants, and places them on the table. Then she picks up a jar from the cluster of ingredients on the bench. She takes out two bay leaves and sits at the table, gesturing for me to do the same. 'You can use these for wishes,' she says, holding them out.

I sit up a bit straighter.

'You can write a wish on a bay leaf. Sometimes people burn them, but I like to let them sit in the food, and then the whole meal is a kind of spell. Do you have anything you want to wish for?'

My mind runs blank. I've already wished for friends. There are probably a million things I would wish for, like to do okay at school. But I don't know what to choose right now.

'It's okay. We can leave it more general for today,' she says and gets out a safety pin that was tucked away somewhere in her outfit. She hands it and a bay leaf to me. 'Just write something like, *This meal will be fulfilling.*'

I scratch out the letters, lightly enough that they make a mark but not so hard that they tear a hole in the leaf. *This meal will be fulfilling*, I write, stumbling over the curves in the s and the m.

'Pop it into the pot,' she says.

When I do, the water sparkles the tiniest bit. It definitely wasn't a trick of the light: it was like diamond dust sprinkled out from under my fingers, rippling through the water as the leaf hit. Wendy wasn't looking, she was picking some thyme off the stem, so I can't ask if she saw it too.

'And then these are just a few herbs,' she says, showing me the ones she picked from the wall garden. 'Basically, all plants have some kind of meaning. Some meanings won't make sense to you, so if you think they're different to what I tell you, then that's okay.' She tears the basil leaves off the stalk she picks, then tears them into a few pieces. The smell hits me and I breathe deeply. 'Basil is for protection.'

I know that makes sense.

Thyme she uses for stability; oregano is also for protection. 'I'm big on protection spells,' she says, sprinkling the herbs into the pot. 'Mostly customers want love spells, or to help cure a sickness.' She stirs the pot with a wooden spoon. 'I like to start with seven clockwise stirs, just to get things rolling.'

We sit back down, and she produces more tea – though I didn't see her put on the kettle or make a new pot.

'Love spells are a tricky thing. I can make a spell to help someone create a new space in their life to welcome someone else in, but I could never trick someone into falling in love. And with healing spells, they should never replace medicine. They can help things along, but my advice to you is never say that magic will make everything better.'

'I guess that would be too much to hope for.'

She nods. 'People want easy solutions a lot of the time when they come to me. But magic is very subtle, it's like a tiny nudge in the right direction. It's more about getting someone to think about what choices and actions they need to make, for the thing they want happen. Sometimes the action that spurs them into gear is just wanting to see a witch. By the time my spell gets to them, they've already started doing what they need to do. Then the spell is inconsequential.'

'Okay. So basically … it's about realising what you want. Or what other people want.'

She nods.

Babs appears, fresh out of the shower. Her hair is tied up in a bun on her head, wet strands sticking out of it.

She's got a matching set of clothes to me, blue jeans and grey jumpers. Hers has a slogan, THIS MUST BE MY DREAM, in a plain black font. 'Learning?' she asks, sitting down and pouring herself a cup of tea. She spoons in honey but doesn't have any milk. I can smell it's an Earl Grey this time.

'Trying.'

Wendy stands up. 'You're *doing*. I'll get you some books.' She rummages through the shelves and gives me two slim volumes. One is about spellcraft, the other, crystals. I think of the book I found in the op-shop box, tucked in my bag. 'You can keep the crystal one,' she says. 'I don't like them but I think they'll be good for you.'

The rose quartz vibrates against my chest when I touch the book. 'Thank you so much.'

She pats my arm. 'Any time. You read them through, and if you have any questions let me know.'

'I found this book,' I say, bringing it out of my bag. 'It was humming at me.'

Wendy takes the old book with two hands. 'Goodness.' She flicks through the pages. 'This is very special, keep it safe.' Now she turns to Babs, her frame sagging, revealing how tired she is. Her eyes have bags under them, suddenly very pronounced. 'I'm going to have a nap before dinner, can you keep an eye on things? It's the same as last week, just make sure nothing burns, keep the water topped up.'

Babs nods. 'Mum, I've been making bolognese since I was like, seven.'

'I know, I know. Wake me if you need anything, okay?'

'Okay,' Babs says, but I know she would only wake her if it was an emergency. Once Wendy is in her bedroom, the door closed, Babs leans in to me. 'Can I see the book?'

'Yeah!' I lay it on the table, opening its pages so a spread near the middle faces out.

'They're all blank.' Babs flips through. 'Are they blank to you?'

I nod.

'That's so strange. If anything appears, tell me, yeah? I want to know more!' She grins. 'Anyway, I reckon Mum is gonna go to sleep for the night. If it gets too late, we'll just start eating, if that's okay?'

'That's fine,' I say with a reassuring smile.

We do end up eating by ourselves, so we sit on Babs's bed and watch a movie on her laptop. When Moss comes to pick me up later, I tell her about the food and the spells, and she nods, takes it all in. 'Clover probably has some herbs you can use,' she says. I nod, and remember the huge patch of sage near the roses; Clover planted heaps of it to attract bees.

Once Moss and Clover have gone to bed, I slip out of my window and into the garden. I've only got a singlet and undies on, and the grass is cool and wet under my feet. The air is warm, but not enough to stop the little shivers on my skin. Our solar-powered fairy lights, strung up everywhere, still have some charge left from the sun. And the moon is full, which I can only take as a good sign. It lights up the roses, and the other plants Clover included to make sure that flowers would bloom even in the night, like the big bush with curly white bells hanging from it.

I see peach glitter, then Saltkin appears, slightly ruffled. 'Sprout,' he says, 'you're sparking.'

I hold up an arm, and a few white flecks of light come off me. 'Oh my gosh.' I raise my arm again, but nothing happens.

'You've only got a bit at the moment,' he says, perching on a flower near my face. 'She's unlocked you. You'll get colours too, not just light. But not for a while.'

'I thought you said my magic wouldn't be like yours?'

'It's usually not – only some humans can do this. Faeries are born into it, so it's easier for us. But sometimes one of your kind slips through.'

'Is this because we're friends? Did I catch it from you?'

'No,' he says. 'This is all you. Maybe that's why I was drawn to you in the first place? But it's not because of that now. Remember that, okay?'

'Okay.' I nod. 'So, what does this mean?'

'I'm not sure,' he says, thinking. 'You need a teacher. Wendy could do it.'

'I think she has enough on her plate.'

'Hmm.' Saltkin hovers. 'I'll look around.'

'Wendy said I should learn more about crystals.'

'Oh yes, I could tell. I'm glad you like the rose quartz. It's so heavy!' He laughs, delighted. 'It loves you. She was absolutely right. The smoky quartz from the forest loves you as well.'

'I feel like they would appreciate the rope.'

'I should hope so.' He laughs again. 'That took a long time to make, and with the forest being the way it is ...'

'Are you okay, Saltkin?' I ask him.

'You shouldn't ask me that right now,' he says. 'It's not safe. You're just a baby.'

'I'm sixteen!'

He's holding up his hands in apology. 'In faerie terms, you are. I'm over a hundred years old, Sprout.' He's never told me this before.

'Is something out there?' I ask.

'Yes.'

'What is it?'

He ponders his words. 'Anger. Hurt.'

I sigh. 'Fine.'

'I just want you to be safe.' He gets up off the flower and hovers around my head.

'If there's something out there that could hurt me, I want to know all the details.'

'Some things in this world are too dangerous for you to know too much about,' he says. 'It would be harmful for me to tell you.'

'Could I find out on my own?'

75

'Yes.'

'If I did, could we talk about it?'

'Iris, I don't want you to go looking for this danger.' He takes my index finger in his hands imploringly. 'Please don't go looking.'

'Fine,' I say. 'I will try not to go looking.'

'Iris!' he says, squeezing my finger. 'Please!'

'Okay. I promise.'

Sparks fly out around us, my pale white and his peach. He gasps. 'Oh no.'

'What was that?'

'If you make a promise to a faerie, sometimes this happens. It's a bond. Do not break it.' His peach dulls, as though the dye of him is running into water. 'I'm sorry, Iris.'

I've never seen him like this. 'What'll happen if I *do* break it?'

'Don't do that, Iris. It's extremely dangerous. I didn't mean to cast it on you, sometimes it just happens on its own.' Suddenly he looks all of his hundred years, and he curses; I don't speak the language, but I can tell he's swearing. 'It's not safe for you out there.'

'Okay, okay. Fine.' I sigh. He's too good at avoiding the truth. 'Can you help me find some ingredients for a spell? I'm not sure which plant is which.'

He perks up and immediately looks how he used to: young, but not really any particular age. 'What do you need?'

We wander around finding sage, chilli, basil, rose petals. I place them on the outside table and go into the kitchen to get some other things that I know are inside. I consider grabbing the op-shop book as well, but right now I like having it as my secret, even from Saltkin.

When I get back outside, I light the tea candle and start to put everything into a little bottle I found in the cupboard. Saltkin sits beside the candle, his back to it. His wings sparkle in the flickering light, and he makes waves of glitter sparkle out across the table.

Peppercorns to give a fiery spell more passion. Sesame seeds I just grabbed because I like the symbolism of having something with so much potential in a tiny form. I put the garden ingredients into the bottle as well, then I sit and wait for the candle's wax to melt completely.

I wonder if Babs needs to use matches, or if she can make fire just with her hands. Probably just with her hands.

I pick up the candle and it starts sparking, pale white. I put the cork in the bottle and then pour the wax onto it, sealing all the ingredients inside. The wax starts to harden and cool as soon as I tip it onto the bottle, and it blobs onto the table. My fingers are staticky as I pick it up and look at the insides. 'Do you always feel like this?' I ask Saltkin.

'I'm not sure,' he says. 'I don't know what you're feeling.' He laughs. 'This is magic, Iris. It should feel good.'

'It does.' I put down the bottle, and already I miss the tingling in my fingers.

'So, what was it for?' Saltkin asks, gathering up the herbs I dropped on the table. He places them into the empty candle casing.

'Protection, good will, just a general ... goodness. I think.'

'That's what it feels like.' He pats the bottle, which comes up to his hips. 'This is great, sprout. You did very well.'

I smile, then yawn.

'You should rest,' he says. 'You have school tomorrow.'

I nod, yawning again. When I pick up the bottle this time, it doesn't sparkle. I pull myself into bed, and Saltkin makes a nest for himself out of a jumper I left lying on the doona.

Chapter Eight
The Party in the Trees

The boy sees me as I get off the bus, and I wave at him. He's getting off the train, chewing on an apple. We hug and start towards the cafe.

He asks, 'Do you need a hand with something?'

I've got a backpack on, filled to the brim, and my picnic basket is heavy as. 'I got it.'

'What's this all about? A picnic?'

'You'll see. The trees will reveal everything.' I wiggle my eyebrows. 'It's a secret. Careful of the pothole.'

As soon as I finish speaking, the boy stumbles on the hole in the path. 'Have you lived here your whole life?' he asks.

'Yeah. Well, no.' I frown. 'The part that matters, I've been here.'

'I've never lived somewhere like this.' He holds up the apple core. 'Do you know where a bin is?'

'Here.' I piff it into someone's garden. 'It'll be good for the earth, don't worry. Worms will love it. What do you mean, anyway, by a place like this?'

He shrugs. 'I dunno. With like, trees and stuff.'

'Huh.'

'Our school is like five minutes from a national park. And you can disappear! What else is there?' He smiles at me. 'I feel like anything could happen.'

I laugh. 'There's so much more, you just have to wait.'

When we get to the main street, we pause at the public toilets.

'I'll just be a sec,' he says, and dashes in.

'You don't want to use these, they're disgusting,' I call through the door. 'The cafe's got a toilet!'

'I'm not peeing, I just need to change.'

When he comes out, he's wearing a binder. His shoulders are squared, not hunched in like at school. He's standing taller, and when he smiles it feels more relaxed.

'You look good,' I say, and he blushes rose-pink. I want to ask why he doesn't wear it at home, but not yet.

Iris is already sitting inside Eaglefern. They've got a hot chocolate, and they've ordered us a tea and a coffee. When the boy sits next to me on the couch, his shorts ride up a little and I can see some markings. Me and Iris lean in to get a better look.

'Is that real?' Iris asks.

He pulls up his shorts to reveal a geometrical pattern, triangles and stars and loops folding in on each other, tattooed on his thigh. 'I did it,' he says in his quiet, measured voice. 'Stick and poke. I haven't shown my dad yet, dunno how he'd feel. I should probably get longer shorts.' He grins.

'What's stick and poke?' I ask.

'Tattooing but without the gun. Like, you use the same needle but you just poke it into the skin instead of the tattoo gun doing it for you.'

'Oh!' My body lights up like a match. 'Like your rose on your arm. Have you ever done it on anyone else?'

'A couple times, yeah, at my old school. We moved here because Dad got a cool job.'

'I don't know if I've met anyone with a dad,' I say. I don't really know a lot of people, but then I can't think of a time I've met a dad since mine left.

'You don't have dads?' The boy looks between us.

'I have a mum, and Iris has two. It's very strange that you have a dad.'

He laughs. 'He's a very good dad, if that helps.'

Iris grins. 'It definitely helps.'

Livia brings over the cappuccino for me and a soy chai for the boy, honey on the side of the saucer. 'I'll pop back and have a chat in a moment,' she tells us, rushing off to deal with other customers.

The honey slides over the boy's spoon, slow and sticky, as he holds it above the teacup. 'I love tea,' he says when he catches us watching him. 'The whole ritual of it. We have a lot of different teas at home, I should show you one day.'

'That'd be nice. Clover loves tea. I'll show you her collection. Plus, Babs, I've been to your house a few times and it's my turn, I think.' Iris taps their nose, and

I reach up to my own to find a bit of cappuccino froth there. They grin as I wipe it away. 'And I can show you the garden, and the moon roses.'

'Why are they moon roses?' I ask. 'Are they lesbians?'

'What?' Both the boy and Iris look at me in confusion.

'The moon is a lesbian,' I say. 'Have you really not heard this before?'

They're both still looking at me blankly.

I sigh. 'Oh, my sweet children. The moon is a lesbian and she is also trans. Never forget.'

'Makes sense.' Iris nods. 'The moon roses – I don't know if they are lesbians – they glow under the moon at night. Next full moon we can have a sleepover, then you'll see.'

Livia wanders over. 'How you goin', Babsy?' she asks. 'How's your mum?'

'She's, you know. Bit better lately, I think. She's been going out more, too.'

'How's school?'

'It's good.' I gesture to Iris and the boy. 'They can see me.'

'All the time?'

I shake my head. A customer walks in, and Livia goes back up the front.

'Livia can always see me,' I tell the boy. 'That's why I come here when I know no one's going to be able to see me at school. Gets lonely.'

'I kind of understand,' Iris says. 'I feel like no one

knows who I am, really. You see me. It's different but …
I kind of get it.'

'You knew about me,' the boy says. 'Without even
speaking to me. How?'

'Dunno. Magic, maybe.' I shrug. 'Or I recognised
something in you that reminded me of me.' I tell Iris,
'That's why I started talking to you.'

They blush. 'All right. Well, shall we go then?'

Livia gives us a discount on our drinks, and we start off
for the forest. The boy's never been to a forest before – he
says he doesn't really go out exploring the world.

We head down across the road and follow the tiny
creek behind the petrol station and the train station.
It starts to twist and turn, away from the railway and
into the forest. Eventually the road turns from bitumen
to dirt, then it tapers off into a path that looks like it
was made by animals. It's winding, and the trees are
slowly bending in the breeze. The birdsong sounds
out like church bells, constant, everywhere, as they flit
across the canopy. I can hear that some are magpies.
There are butterflies, more than I've ever seen, on every
trunk, all different colours. Black with blue, yellow
and red, and there are orange ones, and lots of tiny
white ones.

The forest is murmuring, rustling, like something's
going to happen. I turn to look at the others. The boy

seems wary – not in a panicked way, just like he doesn't really get what's going on. Here's a boy, not sure of his name or what he is made of. Iris, eyes wide with wonder, is touching the plants either side of the path as we walk by. Iris grew from a seed under moss, brimming with new magic. Their mothers chose their name, and they've grown strong, like the moon roses.

And me, the fiery mess of a girl, crackling when I walk. I forged my own name. I'm invisible sometimes, but I know who I am.

He just needs time. I hope he knows that.

'How far is it?' the boy asks.

'Hard to say. Sometimes it takes five minutes, but the longest it's taken is three hours.'

'Like the bus stop,' Iris says. 'Does yours ever move?'

'Sure. All the time. Sometimes I can't find it, so I just stay home from school.'

The boy's frowning, just a little bit. 'It seems very … odd.'

Iris laughs like a light breeze, wending through tree trunks. 'It is a bit odd.'

'Right. And Livia can see you all the time, though?' he says.

I get the feeling he'd like to be able to vanish sometimes, the way I do.

'Not by choice, but yeah. Livia, Bec and Mum are the only ones who can see me all the time. Bec is the other person who works in Eaglefern. She's really cool. She's studying to be an engineer at uni, and her hair changes colour all the time.'

'Is she a witch too?' Iris asks.

'Reckon so. She's always wearing crystals and has a tattoo of the lunar cycle on her arm.'

'What's magic about the moon?' the boy asks.

'I think it's about cycles, like growth and then a time of rest. It's just ...' I don't know if I know how to explain it. 'I'm not sure. I just love the moon. You can use its light in spells. The full moon and the new moon are both cleansing.'

'My period always syncs to the moon,' he says. 'Almost every time.'

'Mine used to sometimes,' Iris says. 'But then I started taking the pill so I wouldn't get it anymore.'

'I think I should do that,' he says. 'I can't stand getting it.'

'I know a good doctor, if you want me to come.'

He smiles at Iris. 'Thanks.'

We get to a pass, rocks suddenly towering over us on either side.

'Oh!' I say when I realise where we are. 'Hasn't taken long at all, we're almost there. It's not long after this, just be careful. If anyone talks to you, don't trust them. Stay with me.' I take the boy's hand, telling him and Iris to link up as well. 'We can't break the chain, okay?'

The boy looks at me, eyes wide. 'Okay.'

When we start through the pass, right away the temperature drops. I think part of it is from being between two rocks, cool and away from the sun, but no breeze gets through here either. The cold fae live here. They usually stay in the other realm, but lately they've been leaking through more and more.

Sometimes they're kind. They can be very cruel.

There's a hiss, past my ear. Sounds like it's coming from the rock. Iris stops closer to it, but I tug the boy's hand. 'Don't do it, Iris,' I say. 'It's a trick.' They're the kind of faeries that'll take you for what seems like ten minutes, but it's been years.

The sun goes out, and the boy grips my hand. I grip it right back, knot-tight. I can feel a tall, spindly creature beside us. Its limbs are so long, like a spider's; it crouches as it walks. It's blue-grey like a storm cloud. I can't see it with my eyes, but I know what it looks like. The coldest vacuum comes from it, trying to suck us up. It keeps pace with us, side by side with the boy, and I just keep pulling us along.

A tiny ray of sunlight breaks through, then the dark is gone. The spindle creature is gone, and we're out of the pass.

'It's not usually like that,' I say, trying to keep my hands from shaking. 'I'm so sorry.' I'll have to ask Nova why so many are out here.

The boy still hasn't let go of my hand.

'It's never gone dark before, I didn't know they could do that. We can go another way home. It takes longer, but there's a bus back to town.'

'That sounds better,' he says. He goes to sit a little away from us, on a fallen log, to catch his breath, find himself again.

'What was that?' Iris asks me.

'Cold fae. I didn't know they'd be so interested in us. Usually I can feel them a bit, but like, that one was so close.'

'Maybe it was me.'

'You can see them, can't you?'

'Yeah, but I've never seen them before.' Iris shudders. 'I don't know why.'

'Have you been in the realm a lot?'

'Um.'

'That'd be why, they don't cross to our world heaps.'

'Scary.' But they're smiling. 'I've never met anyone who could see faeries. I've been keeping it secret my whole life.'

I don't know what to say to that, so I grab them into a hug.

When we let go, Iris smiles again. 'So, where are you taking us?'

'It's amazing. You'll love it, both of you.'

We walk for a few more minutes, and the boy recovers as we start to come across flowers growing between the trees. These are like the ones in the meadow, glowing softly under the sun. Some of them are small and in tiny bunches, like clusters of stars. Others are yellow, orange, peach – then every colour, some I didn't know flowers could be. The bright-blue ones, like cornflowers, shimmer like an oil-slicked road.

The butterflies are back. They swarm all over me, tickling my face, their tiny tornados ruffling my hair. I put the basket down, raise my hands. Some land on my fingers, and I can't help but laugh, twirl, forget that anything else exists. But the butterflies have to move on, and so I bend to pick up the basket. As we keep going, the flowers and the butterflies become more dense. The trees are still eucalypts, there are still tree ferns, but it's a different kind of forest. Dew glitters like crystals over everything, setting off rainbows.

Eventually, I realise Nova is walking towards us through the trees. Their camouflage is almost too good. 'Babs,' they say on the wind, 'it's ready for you.'

I grin at the others, knowing they're going to love it. 'This is Nova. They're a dryad.'

The boy swallows. 'I can see that.'

'You're from very far away,' Nova says. 'You miss your roots.'

He nods.

'And you know Vada,' Nova says to Iris. They pause

to breathe and sway. 'They told me all about you. You're very lucky.'

Iris nods, but I can see they've got no idea what Nova is talking about.

'Come.' They gesture, wood creaking.

'Did you, er, know that this would happen?' the boy asks Iris. 'Like you can see the tree person. Right?'

'I can. I've met another one before – that's Vada. I've known them for a long time. They helped me realise what my gender was.'

'A *tree*?'

'They're dryads. But they don't have human genders.'

'Well, that makes sense. Why would they.' He laughs and pinches himself. 'I hope this is real.'

'This is totally real,' I say.

'I can introduce you to Vada. Or the faeries that live in my garden. Well, Clover's garden.'

'Faeries?' He raises his eyebrows.

'You just learned dryads are real,' I remind him. 'Plus the cold fae you just felt.'

'Good point.'

We come to a clearing that overlooks the river – very blue, and very sparkling. I feel like it's not exactly made of water. Nova will never give me a straight answer about it.

In the middle of the clearing are a few tables that look like they were grown from the earth. There's bunting strung between the trees, and there are hundreds of balloons in every shade of green.

'It's a birthday party!' I clap my hands, can't help it. 'Because we've never had our own ones, really.' I take the basket to a table and start unloading the food and plates and things.

'Babs! How did you do all this?' Iris asks. 'Everything from my drawing is here.'

All the food they drew is here, or I tried to make sure it all was. The boy had green balloons covering his entire page, and now he's staring up at the real ones. I take his hand, and he squeezes mine briefly. 'Let's eat,' he says, grinning more hugely than I've ever seen him do. Piece by piece, he can build himself, like we did.

As we sit, a few creatures join us. There's another dryad I don't know, and Vada comes along. They're busy in deep conversation with the unknown dryad and Nova, and they wave at Iris. There's also a whole cluster of faeries, and some of them come up to say hello to Iris. They introduce me to Saltkin, the faerie who was in art class. And there's another one, Zinnia, who is rosy shades of red and deep pink. Zinnia flits around like a butterfly, jerky-sharp movements. Then there are other creatures I haven't met, and I don't know what exactly they are, but I asked Nova to invite everyone.

'I can't believe this is real,' the boy says. 'Babs, everything's delicious. Wait!' He puts down his fork. 'Aren't you like, not supposed to eat faerie food? Could we get trapped here?'

'It wouldn't be so bad,' I say, grinning. 'But me and Mum made it all, so it's okay.'

'Okay.' He picks up some fairy bread. Hundreds and thousands are stuck to the sides of his mouth as he eats.

'We should do cake,' I say after a while.

We're the only ones who know the song. Iris and the boy both have lovely voices, ones that loop and brush up against each other in sweet fairy-floss harmonies.

I pick up the knife and hand it to the boy. 'You go. You're the youngest.' I'm not sure when the other two were born, but the boy is so green and fresh. When he cuts the cake, the little chocolate drops spill out from the middle, like a rainbow volcano. As we eat, popping noises come out of our open mouths.

Saltkin flies over to us, pinballing back and forth, clouds of peach fog following him.

'Saltkin!' Iris laughs and he plays with their hair. 'What's happening?'

'This!' Peach-coloured sparkles join the clouds. 'The spell worked, it worked so well!'

'Saltkin helped me with a spell for friends,' Iris tells us.

Saltkin reaches out and takes a handful of Iris's cake. 'I'm so glad you found them,' he says to Iris.

'How much of Babs's food did you eat today?'

'So much.' He turns to me, bows his head. 'You and your mother are very good bakers. Thank you.'

I nod back. 'Any time.'

He flies away to speak with someone else, then we lie

in the sun next to the river. I know this sun won't burn us, somehow, and it's peaceful. Butterflies land on me, and I see fat purple-headed bumblebees on the shining flowers nearby.

I close my eyes. I knew this would be a good idea.

Chapter Nine
The Story of the Sun and the Moon

The day Clover and Moss met, the moon was full and in the sky in the middle of the day. So was the sun, but that was more usual. Clover was sitting in a cafe, or rather she was sitting in the backyard of a cafe, shoes off. She had a pot of tea next to her and a book in her hands.

Moss says it was like walking into a dream. Clover's dress was spread out all around her. It was the middle of summer and the cicadas were just the right amount of loud. The flowers in the garden all seemed to lean towards her.

Clover looked up as Moss walked over, her bright brown eyes like pools of chocolate.

'Are you Clover?' Moss asked. They were supposed to be meeting a friend there, who was running late. Moss knew the friend would be late, but she couldn't bring herself to be late as well. Even though she knew Clover was coming and they hadn't met before, which made her stomach flip and turn.

Clover nodded and patted the grass next to her. 'Or would you like a chair? I just thought the lawn looked too good not to sit on.'

Moss couldn't understand this way of thinking at all, and she hadn't sat on a lawn since maybe primary school. But she sat, and she took off her shoes, just like Clover.

'How do you know Lisa?' Clover asked as Moss undid her shoelaces with a precision that Clover later told Iris she thought was too cute.

'I'm not sure,' Moss confessed. 'I feel like one day she just appeared in my life, like magic.'

Clover nodded. 'I understand that. I can remember a time before she was in my life, but I can't pinpoint when she entered it.'

Moss laughed, and she noticed how Clover's face lit up at the noise.

One of the staff came out with Moss's coffee, black. She took a sip, sighed with satisfaction and closed her eyes.

Clover remembers at this point it was like time stopped.

'This place is so lovely,' Moss said, 'and I live close by. Why haven't I come here before?'

'Maybe Lisa dreamed it up,' Clover said, pouring herself a new cup of tea. The brown liquid sparkled in the sun as Moss watched her.

Moss noticed that her stomach had stopped churning; now it was alive with butterflies.

They kept chatting, and then Lisa arrived. She'd been on a tram that had broken down. She'd got a lift from someone, but they'd heard the suburb wrong, so then she had to backtrack to a train station. On the way she'd seen a friend she hadn't seen in years, and they had got talking. Eventually she'd hopped in a taxi and made it to the cafe.

Clover thought the most unbelievable part was that Lisa had only been an hour late, and she said so.

'Well, me too!' Lisa exclaimed, and she told them she'd been on the way to be early. 'The universe must have conspired against me, because I'm never on time. I couldn't upset the established pattern, you see.'

'Maybe that's why time stopped,' Moss said.

Clover looked at her in surprise, because she had been thinking the same thing.

Lisa, catching the looks between them, was glad she'd been so late. Maybe she should have been later, she thought, but she stayed for one coffee. Lisa has told Iris that she had a feeling they would like each other. But she hadn't known that Moss was a lesbian, so it wasn't like she was necessarily trying to set them up. (Moss hadn't known either, until that day, and then it seemed as obvious as the existence of the sky.) Lisa just knew there'd be a nice connection there; whatever it turned out to be, it would be nice.

Clover and Moss went to pay for their drinks. By this time Lisa had left, but they discovered she'd paid for everything. So they both still had a little money – they were both studying and working jobs that gave them just enough to get by – and they walked down to the ice-cream shop. They each got strawberry, and then they kept walking together. They weren't sure where they were going, and they ended up walking along a forest path. Tiny star-like flowers were dotted along the ground, pink and purple and blue.

Moss hadn't known that this forest existed so close to her house; it was as if it had just sprung up that morning to make sure she'd have somewhere nice to walk with this girl who was turning into her sun.

Clover noticed that Moss was dressed like the moon, and she said so. Silver and grey and black, that was what Moss was wearing.

Moss realised that Clover's dress wasn't white but rather a pale yellow, and her earrings were sparkling orbs of light.

They walked until the forest ended, and the path led straight to Moss's house. Clover stayed there that night, and she rose with the sun the next morning. Moss was woken by the smell of coffee coming from the kitchen. They both had to go to work soon after, so they caught the train together. Clover took Moss's hand during the journey, and a whole new world awoke in Moss. It was like fireworks were coming from her chest.

As Clover was getting off at her station, they made plans to see each other in a few days. And then that day they made plans to see each other in a few days, and then that day they made plans to see each other the next day. And then they became near inseparable, each in the orbit of her own life, but grounded by the gravity that kept them close.

They moved in together, and they graduated from their courses. That was separate; Clover graduated the year after Moss. Moss got a job as an electrician, and Clover got a job in a bakery nearby. And they were good jobs, and then they had enough to buy the tiny house with a huge garden so far from the city.

Moss fixed up the house, changing the electrics, putting in a new shower, repainting the outside and the in. Clover had always loved plants, and Moss was right about how the flowers all turned to face her: she was warmer than the sun to them, and to Moss. So Clover grew and nurtured their favourite plants, as well as a veggie patch.

Clover adored the huge wisteria in the front yard, and Moss built a table for them to sit at on the warmer nights, and they would have dinner there. They still have dinner out there sometimes with Iris.

Moss got a promotion, and then Clover lay awake at night. She could feel something had changed. The house was warmer, the plants were happier, the food was more wholesome, Moss's coffee in the morning made her more awake. And then Clover realised something was growing in the garden under the moss.

At first she was unsure of what it was, but she asked the insects and the rabbits and everything else to stay away from the garden bed covered in moss. They did, but they never ate her plants anyway. Well, only a little bit. Things she could afford to give away. They never ate anything so that it died, or so that Clover and Moss went hungry.

And then a few weeks later, as they were both sitting outside under the light of the full moon, drinking tea and chatting about nothing, Clover realised that under the ground, under the moss, in the safe dark, was Iris, and they were growing.

She gasped, then she started crying.

'Clover?' Moss asked, putting down her cup. 'Are you all right? What's wrong?'

She took her hand, and Clover couldn't stop crying. She was more scared than she had ever been in her whole life, she told Iris later, but she was also happier. It was like she was made of clouds and light, up higher in the sky than she had been before.

'We're going to have a baby,' she said, her whole body shaking with the effort to hold this many emotions at once, and still speak.

'A baby?' Moss repeated, unable to believe that they could have something so precious and small and new. 'A real baby?' she asked, and whenever she tells Iris now that she asked this, she laughs. She says she couldn't have said anything sillier.

'A real baby,' Clover said, and then she couldn't talk from the deluge of feelings that rocked her body.

They left the tea out as they went inside, and they lay in the moonlight the whole night, melding into one another.

Chapter Ten
The Strange News

I'm in that murky fog of sleep when something wakes me. I groan and turn over, but the thing keeps nudging me.

'What, Sadie?' I mumble, creaking open an eye.

It's not Sadie. It's a ... I don't know what they are. At first they look like a bird, but the lines are wavy, shimmery ... then a faerie ... then just a bundle of sticks. As I open both eyes, they stabilise into a raven. We stare at each other.

'Hello,' I say.

The raven caws.

'Are you looking for my mum? She's in the other room.' Sadie's probably in with her.

The raven caws again.

I sigh. 'Fine.' I swing my legs out of bed, make a doona cape and head to the bathroom.

The raven caws.

'Yeah, yeah, just give me a sec, okay?'

I shower and look at my hair. Mum's got colouring potions in the cupboard – she did some for a client a couple weeks ago, and these are the leftovers. A musk smell wafts out when I open the biggest jar. I part my hair down the middle, rub the dye into half. It takes a few minutes to set, so I put on some eyeliner, a pearlescent white, while I wait. I draw thin lines above my eyes, birds on my cheeks. As I do, I watch the brown hair turn to purple, turn to pink.

'All right,' I say to the raven as I'm tying my shoelaces. 'I'm ready.'

The raven flies out my window and waits for me in the backyard. Maybe it's come from Nova. Sometimes they'll send messengers, but almost always to Mum. I've never got a raven-faerie-stick doll messenger, though.

As I step out into the national park, something in my gut twists. 'Where are you taking me?' I ask the raven, but they don't reply. 'I have to be back in time to go to my friend's for dinner, okay?'

No reply.

I roll my eyes. Fine.

So I keep trudging through the trees, my tummy not happy about it. But if Nova's sent someone to get me, it must be important.

The forest is moving with something, I don't know what. Maybe if Iris was here, they could tell me what was going on. Instead, I just keep following the raven, trying not to worry too much. It's not working.

My footsteps are dampened and the mist through the trees makes my skin crawl. There's the occasional bird call, but no other noise. I'm alone. I've never been in the forest when it's so quiet.

I walk and walk and walk and I think about telling the raven where they can stick it. Then we suddenly come to the clearing, but the dryad who's here isn't Nova – they've got pine needles and crackly bark. 'Vada?'

'Yes.' The raven flies to Vada where it turns into sticks, reattaches itself to their body. 'I saw you at the party, Babs, and Iris has told me about you.'

I don't know what to say. If I was talking to Nova, I'd maybe have a go about sending ravens for me so early in the morning.

'Nova didn't want me to tell you this, and I wasn't sure if I should. I know you and Iris are finding your place in the world. I thought about telling them, but then I didn't want to give them the burden of deciding to tell you or not – they're too young.' A pause. 'Babs, the witch is here.'

For a moment I'm floating in space, seeing nothing, hearing nothing, feeling like I'm just a mind. Then I come crashing back, my feet pressing into the earth, my muscles pushing me away from it. 'What?'

'I'm not sure when she arrived, but it's been some time.'

'*Something is happening*, that's what the faeries and Nova kept saying.' I try to focus on my breathing, keep it slow. My head feels light, too light.

'I don't know if you're in any danger. But I thought you should know.'

I breathe in through my nose and out through my mouth.

'Nova didn't want me to tell you.'

'They never want to tell me anything.' I spit the words. 'They think I'm a child.'

'They're just trying to protect you.'

'I don't care.' I cross my arms. 'Will you get in trouble?'

'It doesn't matter.'

'Have you seen the witch?' I wonder what she looks like now. Does she know I'm here? Is that why she's here?

'I haven't. She's far away.'

The birds start to sing, the meadow flowers shine their ethereal light.

'Okay.'

'I don't think she means any harm, to you or the forest. But we'll see.'

'Does Nova know you're telling me?'

'Not yet.' They seem to decide something, because then they start herding me away from the meadow. 'I'll walk you back to the path. Try to come to the forest less often.'

'That's not gonna happen.' I ball my fists. 'It's like asking me not to breathe.'

Their eyes crinkle up in a smile. 'Well, be careful.'

In less than five minutes, I step into a backyard brimming with plants. They're spilling from the garden beds and onto the paths. This is Iris's house, and this is Clover's garden. I could spend all day looking at everything, but I want Iris to show me. So I walk up by the fence to the front yard, where I see the boy climbing out of a car. I wave to him, and he smiles in relief. 'I always get worried that somehow I've gone to the wrong place,' he says. He waves to someone in the car – his dad?

'Habibi, the food!' The man gets out, waving around a bag. The boy takes it off him while he shakes my hand. 'I'm Mahmoud,' he says, his grip warm and firm. Immediately, I like him.

'I'm Babs,' I say, smiling.

'Thanks, Dad,' the boy says.

'I'll pick you up later.' Mahmoud kisses the top of his head. 'Be safe.'

As Mahmoud gets back into the car, the boy turns to me. 'Always bring food,' he says, gesturing to the bag. 'That what my dad says. Typical Arab dad.'

'What'd you bring?' I peek at the bag: a whole bunch of things – not Homebrand, either; there are real Doritos. 'Awesome.'

We knock on the door and Iris opens it, eyes wide. 'Hey,' they say, puffing a little. They must've run to the door.

'This is from my dad,' the boy says, offering Iris the bag.

'*Yummm*, thank you.'

We take off our shoes and leave them by the front door. 'Can I make a tea?' I ask. 'It's been ... a strange day.' I swallow. For a second I'd almost forgotten.

'What's up?' Iris asks as they flick on the kettle.

I sit at the table and get my phone out because I can't bear to look them in the eye. I scroll through things without reading them. 'I dunno. I can't say it yet. Soon.'

'All right.' Iris exchanges a look with the boy, who shrugs.

As Iris brings the teacups over, the boy sits opposite me. He sits up straight, shoulders back, looking around the kitchen curiously. He lingers on something behind me. 'Are those the moon roses?' His voice is so steady.

I turn and see some pearly-white roses in a vase on the windowsill.

Iris says, 'Yeah, come on. I'll show you.'

We grab our shoes and tea and head out through the laundry to the backyard. How am I supposed to tell them both that the witch is back, that I don't know if she's hunting me, that maybe it's a coincidence but I'm still scared?

There's no mist here; the sun is gentle and there's a slight breeze, just enough to notice.

Iris takes us to the moon roses, and the boy's face flushes as he looks at them. Iris and I sit down at some rickety metal chairs as the boy wanders around the garden, gaping at all the plants.

'What happened this morning?' Iris asks me.

I take an extra-long sip of tea, Earl Grey with a little lemon. 'I should wait till the boy gets back.'

'When I woke up the air felt different,' they say.

I watch the boy, delicately reaching for flowers and smelling them, moving plants out of the way so he can pass without damaging them.

'Vada told me something,' I say, staring into my cup. I hold it with both hands, clasped firm on either side so I can't tell if I'm shaking or not. Feel like I might be. 'They sent a messenger to take me to the realm this morning.'

'Which one is Vada again?' the boy asks as he sits down with us. He takes a sip of his tea. 'This is perfect, by the way. Love the lemon.'

Iris smiles, but they're still frowning at what I said. 'Vada is the dryad I know,' they say. 'Nova is the one Babs knows, and the one you met.'

'So are they all non-binary?' the boy asks.

Not now, I want to yell, but I don't. I just stare at the tea. *This is important.*

'I don't think so,' Iris says. 'I mean, they all use they pronouns, but they don't have gender in their society, it doesn't make sense to them. Vada said they had to really work a lot to actually understand what humans were talking about when they first made contact.'

'You said before that's how you figured it out?' the boy says.

'Yeah.' Iris frowns when they see my face. 'I thought

about it for a while, then I asked them if humans could be the same as them. And they said not the same, but they told me about how they had known genderqueer people before. Anyway, Babs, what do you need to tell us?'

I smile gratefully. 'It's to do with the forest ...'

They both look at me, wanting me to say more. I don't know if I can.

I shiver. 'Let's go inside.'

Iris takes my hand and leads me to their room; the boy follows with my tea and his. Iris's room is filled with things: rocks, sticks, books, flowers in vases, plants, posters on the walls. The walls are white, but the ceiling is a lovely pea-green. I lie on the bed, and the others sit cross-legged beside me.

There are three ferns on the windowsill. One's a Boston, one's a maidenhair, but I don't know what the last is. It's got dark, delicate leaves. I've never seen a fern like it.

'The witch is in the forest.'

Neither of them say anything.

Iris takes my hand again, rubs their thumbs across my palm. The boy shifts so his leg is pressed against mine.

'I don't know what to do.'

'What do you want?' Iris asks.

'I don't know. I wonder if she could fix me. Or make it worse.'

'Maybe she could. You don't have to do anything now.'

'But she's *here*,' I say. My voice cracks. 'She's here and

she could find me first. Nova didn't want to tell me, but they're supposed to be my friend.'

'They probably just wanted to keep you safe,' says the boy. 'They didn't want you to worry.'

'How am I supposed to prepare for that?!' I remind myself again to breathe slower. I close my eyes. 'Sorry. I shouldn't yell. I'm afraid.'

I feel like I'm a tiny flicker, the dying embers of a fire.

'Why don't we just talk about other things.' I try to make my voice light as birds, but there's a heavy lump in my throat. 'What's for dinner?'

'Roast veggies with feta,' Iris says, 'and other stuff but I've forgotten. Me and Clover went shopping this morning to get everything. She's a great cook.'

That makes me smile, though the lump is still there, getting heavier.

I smile and laugh through dinner, but I'm glad we're not sleeping over tonight. I want to be home so I can tell Mum everything.

Moss drops me off and I thank her. Mum's in the lounge room watching something, Sadie's head resting in her lap. At the doorway I look at her for a few moments, seeing her laugh, clap and sigh.

'Babs!' she says when I start to walk into the room. 'How was Iris's?' She's smiling so much I don't want to tell her.

'Yeah, it was really nice. Their house is so cute, and their mums are nice. But I'm tired, I thought I might go lie down.'

'Sure, sweets.' I lean over so she can kiss my head. 'Your hair looks great.'

In my room I turn off my light and put on the star lamp, the one that rotates the night sky on my walls. I open the window and the warm night breeze drifts through. I touch the wicks of some candles and they flare up not with orange but with my own butter-yellow light. I lie on the floor, watching the stars dance over my bookshelf, the wardrobe, the outline of the door. Maybe I could just stay here forever, watching them.

There's a scratch at the door, and I get up to open it. Sadie walks in, her grey snout pushing into my hand. She huffs at me.

'You're right.' I sigh.

I blow out the candles and climb into bed. She curls up beside me and I listen to her big lungs through the night.

Chapter Eleven
The Deep Water

It's hot, so after school we don't go to the cafe. Instead we catch the train a few stops until we get to the one with the milk bar, near where the boy lives. We haven't been to his house yet, and I'm excited to see what it looks like.

I've got the op-shop book in my bag. Leaving it at home felt a bit off, so I've been keeping it in my schoolbag, in my locker, and then I bring it out at night and look at the blank pages. It's been a couple of weeks since I found it. There must be something there; why else would it call out to me?

The milk bar has all kinds of weird ice creams, ones I've never seen before. They're all rip-off brands, like Roads instead of Streets, and super cheap so me and Babs don't have to worry. I get an icy pole that has ice cream on the inside, Babs gets a cup of vanilla ice cream with a spoon, and the boy gets a fancy one with a chocolate-and-caramel coating.

We sit out the front as we eat them. Me and the boy sit on the windowsill that juts out, and Babs is leaning against the rubbish bin.

'So, what movie are we gonna watch tonight?' she asks. 'I can't do scary movies.'

'We can have a look, my dad has heaps of DVDs.'

The boy's neighbourhood is very respectable, the kind of suburbia I imagine people dream about when they want to get married and have children and take them to a nice school. Everything's pretty clean, and the council gardens are all neat and trimmed. We walk past a primary school with no graffiti on it anywhere.

The boy's front yard has a cute picket fence, a line of neatly trimmed rosebushes behind it. The house looks like it's pretty new; its paint isn't cracked or anything. I wonder why he's going to our school when they could afford something better.

We take our shoes off as we enter. The boy has a wooden shoe rack just inside the door, which I think is very cute.

'Lunchbox!' he calls down the hall.

Babs looks as confused as I feel, but then we hear a jingle and a huge fat ginger cat comes running down the hallway. It runs right up to the boy and purrs so loudly I can hear it as if it was sitting in my lap.

'I named him when I was little,' the boy says, lifting Lunchbox into his arms. He moves closer to us, allowing us to pat the cat if we want. His fur is thick and soft, and he mews in delight as we stroke him. 'Lucky day,

Lunchbox, three people patting you at once.'

The boy puts the cat down and we keep walking along the hallway. It has nice carpet, not worn through. The kitchen seems bare, but when he opens the pantry it's full of food. 'Is anyone hungry?'

'A bit,' I say, because I don't want to eat everything they have. But looking at it all in the pantry, I feel like I could.

'All right.' He puts his bag down and reaches for a big Tupperware container. The lid comes off to reveal some baklava. 'Dad made this yesterday, so it's pretty fresh. Do you like baklava?'

Me and Babs nod so hard I feel like our heads are going to fall off.

He makes us tea as well, and we take it out to a table on the deck, protected by a roof of corrugated clear plastic and covered in lush pot plants. 'Didn't you only just move here?' I ask, staring around at them.

'Yeah, Dad really likes plants, so he went and got all these pretty quick. I mean, it's been a couple months now.'

The house and garden look so perfect and clean. Kind of like an IKEA catalogue.

'Your dad would like Clover,' I say. 'She loves gardening.'

'He'd like you too,' Babs says. 'You big walking plant.' She giggles into her tea.

It starts to rain, but we're safe and dry on the deck.

Through the plastic roof the sky is turning a dark blue; it feels like it's almost night-time. Babs goes inside to use the toilet, and as she comes back out through the sliding glass door, a big roll of thunder tumbles across the sky. The boy and I jump in our seats, while she looks to the sky in wonder. 'Are you going to colour your hair?' she asks the boy. I realise she's holding a tube of dye.

He blushes to his ears. 'I was thinking about it.'

'I think it'll suit you,' she says, nodding. 'Dark fern-green.'

'I'm not sure if Dad will like it.'

'It's okay, only you have to like it,' I say. 'Will he be mad at you?'

'No,' the boy says. 'But I dunno about it.'

'Do you think it'll look good?'

'Maybe. I've been thinking about it for a while.' He gives one of his small smiles. 'I do think it would look good. I've wanted to for ages.'

'Let's do it!' Babs exclaims. 'You wanna bleach your hair first?'

He has black hair so the colour's either going to be really dark, barely noticeable, or if we bleach it first it'll be pretty bright.

'I wanted to just put it over, so like, it's really dark green. I'm not sure if it'll work.'

'We can try,' Babs says. 'Let's do it right now?'

He is hesitant, but he nods.

We finish our tea, watching the rain run in rivulets off the roof and splash onto the ground outside. The day was hot enough that it's still warm on the deck.

Babs and the boy go inside and get everything they need, and when they come back out I help them lay flat some newspapers so no dye gets on the wooden floor or the table. I've never dyed anyone's hair before, not even my own. It seems Babs is an expert on all things hair, because she knew what to do for mine. But I guess mine was pretty straightforward, all shaved off. It's growing in again, and it's fluffier and less spiky and irregular. I'll ask her to do it again soon.

I squeeze the tube of green onto the boy's head. He's changed out of his school uniform, just in case, into some trackie daks and an old t-shirt that looks like it's pyjamas and smells like it's been slept in. Not in a bad way, just in a way that smells like him, and warmth, and night-time.

Lunchbox jumps up onto the table next to the dye, starts licking a paw, as Babs quickly spreads the goop around with a brush.

'Will I get in trouble at school?' the boy asks. Kids have been asked to take out piercings and not dye their hair and not wear jewellery.

'It's probably subtle enough that it won't matter,' Babs says. 'One time I dyed my hair that blue that's basically black and they never told me off.' She doesn't say anything about the pale sugar-pink in at the moment.

'But also,' I point out, squeezing another bit of goop

onto the boy's head when Babs indicates, 'you *are* invisible half the time.'

'You're not wrong,' she says. 'But also. They did see me some of the time.'

'I guess we'll find out tomorrow,' he says. He looks a bit nervous; he's wringing his hands under the table where he thinks no one can see, but his shoulders are squared, determined.

While the dye soaks in we watch some telly. His family has pay TV, so we put on a cooking channel. There's this show about a married couple in the UK who make lollies, and we watch them make some magic-looking honeycomb and chat away to each other about their lives. Their connection runs deep, and their love shows in their food, and then at the end of the episode when they share it with their friends.

I look at Babs and the boy, both captivated by the lollies on screen, and I feel that same kind of warmth for them.

An alarm on Babs's phone goes off: time to rinse out the dye. The bath runs green with it, a dark fern-green like Babs predicted. Then the boy gets out a sleek black hair dryer. My hair's normally too thick to use a dryer properly without spending five hundred years holding it up, but he's done in a couple of seconds, it feels like. When he runs a hand through his hair, it parts like silk, and it's definitely a shade that could be mistaken for black in the right light.

'Exactly what I wanted,' he says, smiling at me and Babs.

Mahmoud has to work late, so we don't get to see him. Babs and I catch the bus home and I get off at the stop before her as usual. Before I get off, she hugs me and gives me a kiss on the cheek.

Tiny flames spark out and warmth spreads to my toes.

She laughs and we wave as she moves away, safe in the belly of the bus, under the blue lights.

I walk home; this time it takes a long, long time, more than I'm used to. Maybe this is the longest it's ever taken.

There's a note on the fridge to say Clover and Moss have gone out for a dinner with a couple of their friends. They could have texted me, but I like how they leave me notes sometimes. There's some leftover red curry in the fridge from last night, and Clover says I can have that or make whatever I want.

I decide on the curry and heat up some garlic bread in the oven as well. I put some rice in the cooker, because there's none left, and wait in the kitchen while everything heats up. It's still raining, and thunder rolls out again. It shakes the glasses in the cupboards, clinking them against one another.

The house is stuffy from the past couple of days' heat, and so I open all the windows. A breeze that smells like electricity and promise runs through the house and combs through my hair, tugs at my limbs. I laugh, spin.

In the kitchen I have the best view of the lightning that crackles across the dark-blue sky, racing through the clouds. A fork hits one of the gum trees in the backyard, and I yelp. It leaves burn marks all the way down the trunk, and flames start up, but they're small. Soon the rain dampens them.

A peach flickering catches my eye, and Saltkin appears in the kitchen after flying through the open back door.

'Hey, Saltkin.' I wish he was large enough for me to hug. 'I found something.'

He cocks his head. 'What?'

'A magic book.' I don't know why I haven't shown him until now. Maybe I'm jealous of his magic; I wanted something secret of my own. But now I want to share. And maybe he can help me fill in all the blank pages.

'What's it about?' he asks.

I dig through my schoolbag and bring it out.

His eyes widen, and he flitters so he's hovering over the book. 'Where did you find this?'

'Under all the free books in the op-shop box. Outside. But like, the box was a lot bigger than it should have been; it was deeper than it looked.'

'This book wanted you to find it. It's very old, and no one's sure who wrote it. Not even sure if it was humans or one of us, or something else. I never thought I would see it again.'

'Again?'

'It pops up every now and then. There are several copies, all gravitating towards magic users. And you're one of us now. It must want you to learn. You have a pure heart, sprout.'

'Is it dangerous?'

'Magic can be used as a weapon, so this book could be used in the same way. But it doesn't have to be. I don't think it would be dangerous for you.'

He sits on the salt shaker opposite me, thinking. Sparks fly out from him, cascading down. His colour moves from orange to pink and back again, in a slow gradient. 'You must be part fey, somewhere,' he says. 'I think that's why. Oh!' He claps his hands together. 'This is wonderful. There's so much for you to learn, Iris!' I laugh as he disappears, joyous, into a cloud of peach sparkles, then reappears. 'The world will open to you in different ways, if the magic is awakening in you.' He disappears again. 'It's like you'll be reborn into a new life, just wait and see.'

A thunderclap rolls out like a long whip, and then lightning scatters all over the sky.

'I have to go,' he says. 'Make sure everyone is okay.' He's still shimmering, though at least he's visible through the cloud of peach. 'You never know, the forest is stirring strangely since the witch came here.' He kisses me on the forehead, and it's like a jolt of static electricity. Then he's gone.

I haven't had a bath in a long time; they take too much water and too much time. Plus I always stay in them too long, and the water gets cold and I get all shivery. But now seems like a good idea, when outside it's storming and dark. I light a few candles, and grab a cold Milo, and draw myself a bath.

I sit on the edge of the tub, dip my feet in. They go further than the bath should, and I move them back and forth. The water is cool, like the dam one of Clover's friends lives near. The water feels like the dam water too, though I'm not sure how I know the difference. The dam has always kind of scared me because it's so deep, but I'm trying not to be afraid anymore.

Goosebumps crawl up my legs. The water becomes greeny-brown as I lower more of myself into it, and it just keeps going. There could be anything down there, I suppose, considering it's not my bathtub now. Platypuses, plants.

I let go of the edge and slip in completely. I'm invisible to everything, I only exist in the quiet of the water. I watch as the air bubbles escape to the surface around me. Eyes open, quiet. Nothing else exists.

As I let myself sink down deeper, my foot brushes against a submerged branch; it jabs me and I draw back, but no blood appears. The skin isn't broken.

Bubbles of silver light float up all around me, and I just keep sinking. There doesn't seem to be a bottom, though I'm not afraid. I don't seem to need to breathe.

I keep sinking, but it doesn't get darker. It's as light as if I was right under the surface.

Something is moving to the right of me. I twirl through the water and see a platypus. It sees me, startles, and swims off. Silver bubbles trail up after it, and I notice ducks swimming on the surface.

Soon my arms start to get goosebumps too, so I swim up. When my head breaks the surface, I'm lying in a shallow bath. The candles flicker on the edge, the rain is still pouring outside, and there are still bubbles on the water.

Chapter Twelve
The Jar Spells

'I don't want to go to school today,' I say to Mum as we're eating our porridge at the kitchen table. 'I have to tell you something.' I put down my spoon, pick it up again. I can't look at Mum so I look out the window, but then I have to look back at her.

'What is it?' she asks as she sprinkles cinnamon over her food, frowning slightly.

'Vada sent for me the other day. They told me that the witch is here.'

'Your witch?' Mum drops her spoon – it clatters on the floor. 'Babs.' She gets up and hugs me. She smells like bed still, warm and comfortable.

I let myself be held while I try to keep calm.

'How are you feeling?' she asks, tears in her eyes.

'Not, uh, not good.' How else can I say it?

'Do you think you're in any danger? We can do some protection spells today.' She sits again, but she leaves her spoon on the floor. 'We can do something. What do you need?'

'I dunno, Mum.'

'Have you been in the realm since Vada told you?'

I don't look at her.

'Babs!'

'I have to live my life!'

'There's a difference between that and being safe.'

'That's victim blaming, and you know it.'

I can see in her face she knows I'm right. 'Just don't go into the realm till we can sort this out.'

'I'm going to do what I want.'

'Babs, please, it's not safe.'

'You're not the boss of me,' I say, then wish I could take it back.

Mum's face hardens, then softens. 'I just want you to be safe, Babs.' She sighs and bends down to pick up the spoon. 'Let's go somewhere, yeah? We can do some shopping.'

I can't finish breakfast so I just go straight to the bathroom to get ready. I make clouds of purple and pink on my cheeks, over my nose, then use white liquid eyeliner to draw a smattering of stars across everything, joining them with connect-the-dots lines. I stare at myself and wonder why a witch would want to curse a child.

She didn't seem mean.

I grab some clothes out of my wardrobe, the softest, billowiest ones. They feel gentle on my skin and I wish I could just float away. My boots are by the door and I tie them to my feet to keep me grounded.

Mum comes out with about a million green shopping bags. I take half and we go to the car. We've had it for as long as I can remember. Old and a bit rusty, but it never fails. I think Mum's done some magic, though she always insists she's just looked after it well. There are still stickers on the back-seat windows from when I was little – the bubble stars and the cartoon characters I didn't recognise, but the stickers were cheap so we got them.

Mum reverses out the driveway onto the road, and we're off.

'Where are we going?' I ask.

'Maybe to the Gate? I'd like to get some of those doughnuts.'

Even though it's not the closest shopping centre, it tends to be the quietest. When we get inside, it smells like lavender. The whole place.

'Mum, it stinks,' I say, wrinkling my nose. 'Can you do something?' She can do this spell that surrounds us with an air bubble. We don't really use it except sometimes when we sneak into the tip to get stuff, but it's handy in places like this.

She shakes her head. 'Sorry, baby, not today. It's pretty bad.'

'Should we sit down?' I see her hand shaking on her cane. 'I want a coffee.'

'All right.'

We sit and Mum reads the newspaper. She hates it,

but she says sometimes you just have to know what other people are reading.

I trace patterns in the chocolate-covered foam of my cappuccino. 'What kind of protection spells can we do?'

Mum has a think before looking up at me. 'We're going to need some supplies. But I've got a few in mind.'

We sit for a while longer and let Mum's painkiller kick in, then we're off. I grab a trolley from the supermarket. We get fresh flowers, some herbs, lots of candles, and a few jars from the two-dollar shop. When we've got everything, we go to the doughnut shop and I order us four: two for now and two for home. I sit at the table and peel the sticky tape back on the paper bag, letting the smell waft out for a moment. 'Which ones do you want now?' I ask, though I know Mum's going to say the banana cream.

She does, and I hand it to her. I get out the pink iced for myself. I bite into the still-warm doughnut, the icing sticky-fresh, and grin at Mum.

'Worth it,' she says.

When we get home, Mum has a nap and I take Sadie for a walk before cleaning the kitchen table. The cookbooks and the fruit bowl and the letters and the tablecloth – I put them all aside and get out the things we bought today.

Mum wants to make jar spells and bury them equal distance apart, around the whole house. Jars are her favourite kind of spells, and I like making them with her. Usually she just tells me what to do because I can't read the spellbooks half the time, and I always forget the ingredients she knows off by heart.

I touch a few of the candles and they light, warming the table just a little. I wash all the jars and make sure their stickers are off, and separate the bundles of herbs into piles.

I message Iris to say I can't come to school today. It's so hard to be visible, I think. And I'm scared, though I don't want to admit it to Mum.

When Mum's awake, I bring her a cup of tea and sit next to her in bed. 'How are you feeling?' I ask her as she sits up.

She looks at me, groans. 'We'll see.' She picks up the tea from the bedside table and takes a sip. She sighs. 'Perfect. I am ... adequate.' She smiles at me. 'Ready to do some magic.'

I hug her, careful of the tea. 'Excellent.'

She puts on her dressing-gown, then we start in the kitchen. I've got out the mortar and pestle, and she tells me which things to crush up. She lights some candles as I grind up some salt, cinnamon, lavender. She comes back to sit at the table with basil leaves.

It takes a while to make enough for all the jars she wants buried around the house, and we stop for lunch halfway. The kitchen smells like cinnamon, warm and rich, and I breathe it in. I don't know how much this will help, but it's nice to be working with Mum. She normally does all this stuff when I'm at school.

'I'll bury them,' I say, once the candle wax is cooled on the outside of the jars. 'I think I should do it.'

She nods. 'All right. I'll clean up and then we can watch a movie?'

I put all the jars in a basket and go out to the shed for the shovel. As soon as I'm through the back door, Sadie barks and bounds over, wanting a pat. The shed is little and rickety, and there's nothing really in it, but Mum still locks it. I trace the sigil on the door, then pull it open. I grab the shovel and some gloves.

The backyard is quiet today, it's a wet spring day and the ground is soft with the night's rain. Three rosellas chitter among themselves in the lemon tree as I walk to the edge of the yard. There's no fence, so I guess where the national park starts and plant the first jar. Sadie helps by digging a hole next to mine. My shovel narrowly misses a few worms and I wince – I don't want to cut one in half. I dig the next hole with my gloved hands. The ground is soft and rich; it's like sticking my hands into flour.

Sadie happily follows me, tail wagging. Sometimes she digs holes, and sometimes she doesn't. I just want to crawl into bed.

I stand up after burying the second jar and stare

out into the trees. Would the witch even remember me? Maybe she's cursed lots of children. Maybe she's thousands of years old and one person means nothing.

My hands turn into fists. How could she not remember? She's changed my life so much. I flicker into invisibility for a second, and when I try to catch myself, I can't hold on.

I guess it doesn't matter because the only person I'm seeing today is Mum, but … it does matter. I cover my mouth with my hands and scream through my teeth – I don't want Mum to hear. It's not fair.

I pick up the basket and my gloves, and keep going.

Chapter Thirteen
The Art Project

'This is the project you'll complete as part of your final assessment for this term,' Miranda says, and she seems pretty excited. I wonder what it'll be, what we'll have to use. She's always either very particular or extremely open in her instructions, and I'm not sure what to expect from her tone. She walks around the room handing out photocopied pieces of paper, and on the first sheet there's the assessment grid all the teachers have to give us. Scorings out of five for originality, dedication, things like that. My marks in art are never really that great for skill, but she always gives me a good enough mark for trying.

Babs walked into the room at the start of class, but she's disappeared since then, so I'm just sitting next to the boy.

'How did you choose your name?' he asks me.

'This is the one my mothers gave me.' I unzip my pencil case and get out a greylead. 'I think they knew, somehow. They said they wouldn't mind if I changed it.'

'That must be nice.'

I frown. 'Is your dad not okay with you?' I can't believe a parent would act like that, though I know that they do.

'No, no, he's fine. I just mean, it's so hard choosing a name. Some people seem to find it so easy, but I just can't seem to find one that fits.'

'You will,' Babs says, appearing. 'I chose this one because I feel like I always knew it was mine, and you'll have that moment too. It's okay. You'll be okay.'

He smiles then exhales a tiny tornado. I wonder if his ribs are big enough for how he feels. His body is radiating something, but I can't tell what. Maybe he is made of fire like Babs, but in a different way.

'It's just … it makes me feel a bit lost, I think.' He gets out his brand-new packet of pencils, different from the coloured ones he had last time, and pierces the plastic. He pulls out the lightest greylead. 'Sometimes I don't feel real.'

Maybe he is made up of the space between the stars, of nothingness, the void. He could be yawning and wide, like the universe. 'You're real,' I say. 'You're real and we're here for you.'

Babs nods at him. 'I might not always be around, like physically, but text me, okay? I can always access that.'

'Unless your battery runs out.' He grins at her.

She laughs, and takes out her bundle of pencils. 'Unless that, yes.'

'Come on, you three,' Miranda says, without any malice.

Babs looks up in surprise, but then gets right to work, sketching out something so rough I can't tell what it is. I pick up the handout and take a look at what we're supposed to do. It's one of her open assignments, worth fifty per cent of our mark, and not due until the end of term. We're supposed to create a folio as well, showing our process and how we chose to do what we did. We can:

1. Make something that represents us, our selves, our souls, our stories.
2. Explore a theme from the list attached, and link it to our own creative process.
3. Choose a favourite song, movie, book, etc., and represent it through art.

The list attached has words like 'love', 'anger', 'sadness': emotions as tiny words. I don't understand how I could put one single emotion into a single work. Each of my emotions is tied to another. Like jigsaw pieces they all fit together, and any one couldn't survive on its own. I don't know if it would mean anything by itself.

So I think about the first suggestion. I know my self, sure. I don't know if I believe in souls; I don't think I do. Clover and Moss are both non-religious and so they brought me up that way too. And my story, I'm not sure what that is.

Grown from a seed?

The third suggestion seems unnecessary. It's already a work of art, why would I make another one?

I draw a line on my sketchpad to represent the ground. I draw a little circle and colour it in, and that's me, as a seed. I get the dark-green pencil and draw a line of moss on top of the other line. It seems very underwhelming. How am I supposed to convey the safety I felt, under the ground? Or the blooming of the moon roses, and how they glow in the night? I tap my pencil against the paper.

Babs has disappeared again, and the boy is deep into his sketch. There are a lot of colours; I'm not sure what he's drawing.

Miranda comes over to me. She sits in the empty chair opposite me, the one next to Babs. It's strange how none of the teachers seem to comment when Babs disappears, or when she doesn't show up to class weeks at a time. 'Having a bit of trouble, Iris?' Miranda smiles. She must be a parent; she has that mum smile. The reassuring one, the one that means safety.

'I'm not sure which one to do.'

'Which one would you like to learn more about? Yourself, your feelings, or the art you like?'

'Myself,' I say right away.

'For me, art is all about learning about yourself. Do you think that's true?'

I shrug. 'I just think it's fun. It's my favourite class. I don't have to think too much.'

'So it's more of a relaxation thing for you?'

'I'm not sure.'

'It's okay.' She smiles the smile again. 'There aren't any wrong answers here. I just want my class to be a place where you can be whoever you need to be.'

I don't know what to say to that. I keep silent.

'From what we've been talking about, I think you should pick option one.'

'I think I was going to. But I tried –' I gesture to my drawing. 'It just seems very ... underwhelming. How can I get the, like, the magic across?'

'Maybe that's something you can explore in your folio. It's a place where I want you to explore your creative process, to really think about the decisions you make while you're creating art.'

'Hm.' I frown. I don't know if I'm capable of that.

'I think your folio would be very interesting,' she says. I do think she says it to everyone, but I also think she means it. She pats the table and stands. 'You can always send me an email if you need any help outside of class. I don't want this to be homework, I'd rather my students only do their work in class, but if you need to, email me about it.'

'I will, thanks.'

She goes off to someone else who looks as lost as I did. I still feel a bit lost, but now it's more okay that I feel this way.

I pick up my pencil again, and I start to write around the picture in the blank space of the sky.

When I was a seed my mothers would tend my soil; they would ask the rabbits and snails and everything else to please stay away from me when I grew, so that they wouldn't eat my tiny green new leaves. I needed a strong beginning. The moss above me was like a blanket. At night, it would keep the warmth in the soil. I was growing through winter, I was born in spring. The nights were long and cold, and sometimes Clover would come sit beside me in her winter jacket, holding a warm steaming cup of hot chocolate. Moss would bring her inside when it got too cold. Sometimes they would sit together, but Moss still had to work when this was happening. Clover worked sometimes, but she had to take a lot of time off to make sure I was okay.

The dawn was pastel when my first leaves came out from the soil. I remember the gasp Clover made when she saw me growing there. I don't think she could believe it. I don't know if she can believe it now. Sometimes I catch her looking at me with the same disbelief.

They planted a rosebush over where I grew, once I was out of the soil. Now it's as tall as me. It grows huge roses every year, the petals thick and delicate. They are a luminescent white; they sparkle in the sunlight if you get close enough, and they shine out under the moon in the night.

I wonder if Miranda will read it and think it's all a metaphor. Possibly. I guess it doesn't matter what she thinks, I know it's real.

That's how I might feel about gender, now. It's

upsetting when people misgender me, but it's exhausting to get upset about it every time. I'm not sure I can do it anymore. Babs knows, the boy knows, my mothers know. The cafe lady knows.

I write all this down, too.

Babs reappears. 'I think I'm disappearing again,' she says, her face straining like she's making an effort to stay visible. 'Meet at Eaglefern later?'

'Yep.' I nod.

The boy looks up, wrenching himself from his work, but Babs is already gone.

'Do you want to go to the cafe after school?' I ask him.

'I'll have to ask my dad.' He smiles softly. 'I would like to.'

The good thing about Clover and Moss is that they don't mind so much where I go, I only really need to check with them if it's somewhere I'd have to be picked up from, or if we're going out. They just want me to tell them where I'm going, so they don't worry.

We spend the rest of art class in silence, and I try to figure out how to capture that magic in the picture. I wonder if maybe I could use actual magic, but then I'm not sure how that would work, and how I'd get away with it without Miranda asking too many questions. I'll ask Saltkin later, or maybe Wendy. Whoever I see first.

Maybe the book would have an answer.

After lunch, I skip maths and hang out in the library, waiting for the bell to ring. I should be doing other homework, but instead I'm trying to figure out how to draw a seed. I borrowed some gardening books, and they've all got lots of pictures but none of them really show the seeds. They just show seedlings, new leaves pushing through dirt. I wonder what I looked like, a tiny seed or a big one, round or pointed. I should ask Clover and Moss, though I don't know if they would have seen me before I was a seedling.

I start to sketch out some leaves breaking through dirt. I can't get the bright fresh green that I want, but I make a note of it for my folio, and keep going. Maybe I could try something else, glitter or cellophane – stick stuff onto it, do something weird. I think Miranda would appreciate that.

The bell that means the end of school sounds out, and I grab my things, head to my locker right before the rush of everyone trying to get their bags out. I don't wait for Babs or the boy, the rush is too much, so I just start walking down the hill, away from school, and then wander up the main road.

It's not Livia at Eaglefern today, but a staff member with short, spiky pale-lavender hair and a lot of earrings. They're wearing a denim vest and their arms are pretty buff. This must be Bec. When they bring over my coffee, I stumble over my thank you, and they smile at me before going back up to the front.

I bring out the old book, and its pages are still blank. It wanted me to find it, Saltkin said so. I know that much. I open to a random page and put my palm flat against the paper. It's rough, thick, old. I start to hum the way the book was humming when I found it. Just one note at first, but then I slip into a song I was listening to.

The pages hum in response. Joy bubbles up in me, and I keep humming, as ink spreads from under my hand across the page. The page stops humming eventually, and so do I. When I take my hand off, a sigil is revealed. The text tells me it's for safe travels to make sure wherever the sigil-wearer goes, they will be protected.

I trace the sigil on the paper with my finger. Normally I draw them on myself with a makeup pencil, but I don't have one with me. Saltkin usually draws them anyway.

I grab a marker out of my pencil case and I start to draw the sigil on my thigh so that my school dress can cover it. When it's complete, a layer of shimmery light flashes across my skin. It kind of feels like pins and needles, but the sensation is so fleeting I don't know if it is real.

I try to hum other pages to life, but none of them want to appear. I put the book back in my bag and run a hand over the sigil. The skin is raised. I look closer; it's scarred into me.

It didn't hurt, but still the thought sends a chill across me like the flash of shimmers.

'Hey!' Babs says. I jump in my seat; she's already

sitting opposite me. I'm not sure when she came in or if she was here this whole time and I just hadn't seen her. She's out of her uniform and has a t-shirt on that says DID YOU DO IT? 'Sorry about art class. I reckon it's going to be a cool project, though. I'm gonna do my favourite song. It's got the cutest girl singing; she has like this clear voice that just really swims over the music, ya know?' Babs continues to tell me about the cute girl singer until her coffee arrives. She stumbles over her thanks to the barista, and even blushes a little bit.

'Is that Bec?' I ask her.

'Yep. She's a lesbian like me. She's really cool, she's in a band with some other people and they sing about queer stuff. We're not old enough to go to their shows – they're always eighteen-plus. But I have their CD, I'll give it to you.'

'I love her hair.'

The bell to the door tinkles and the boy comes in, holding a couple of books close to his chest. He goes up to Bec, orders and comes to sit with us. He's on the couch opposite, his knees close together. It's like he can never relax, and I hope he learns how to. He deserves to take up space. It's a hard thing to learn.

He has an Earl Grey tea; he gets a slice of lemon, too. After a bit, he opens the lid of the pot to check how it's steeping. Then he takes out the leaves, puts them on the saucer, pours himself the tea, pours in some milk, some honey, squeezes in some lemon. His movements are very precise, and I realise that me and Babs are watching him. He blushes when he notices. 'I just like it.'

Babs giggles. 'Yes.'

'Where did you go?' he asks her. 'After art class.'

'I thought I could get through the whole class,' she says, frowning as she looks out the window. 'But then I just couldn't hold on. I did some of my folio, but then I went to the park and lay in the sun and listened to the album my song's on. The one I'm doing my project on,' she explains to the boy. 'Then I came here to see you. I've been thinking about the witch.'

'Saltkin's been very weird,' I tell her. 'He keeps telling me *something's going to happen* but he never says what. Don't know if it's about the witch. I think you both met him in the forest?'

They nod. I'm glad Babs made that birthday party for us, so we wouldn't have to explain anything to the boy. There's none of that doubt that might cloud our friendship. I think he would have believed us, but then what if he hadn't? I wonder how that would feel. I don't know if it would be unreasonable to be upset, when it's more or less widely accepted that none of this exists.

'I don't think I wanna see her,' Babs says. 'She's probably dangerous. She might lift this curse but then she could make everything worse. Plus, if Saltkin got hurt ...'

'I mean, I'm not sure he was talking about her. He just kept saying it was dangerous out there, and that I'm young, and that I should stay safe.'

'I wonder what Vada would say,' Babs says. 'I bet Nova wouldn't tell me anything.'

I can hear Babs is a bit jealous, maybe. I think because Vada is younger than Nova, they're more inclined to share things with me. Nova seems like the kind of dryad to keep more to themself.

'We can look for the dryads later. But I know it can be hard to get them to come to you if you need something; time is different for them.'

'Yeah, you're right.' She frowns again. 'I just don't know what to do.'

'So … this witch cursed you when you were like, a tiny child?' the boy asks before blowing away the steam coming from his cup and then taking a sip.

'Yes.'

'For no reason other than you walked near her cabin?'

'Yes.'

'I feel like you shouldn't go looking for her. If she did this to you when you were a child and you found her by accident, imagine what she'll do when you're much older and intentionally looking for her.'

'He has a very good point,' I tell her.

She nods. 'I don't think I'll do it.'

But she has an uncertainty about her, and her words are shaky like leaves in the breeze.

Chapter Fourteen
The Old Book

A few days later, there's a butterfly-light knock on the door. When I open it the boy and his dad are here, the boy holding a plate of little sticky cakes. He smiles at me, and I can feel my fire in him.

Mahmoud smiles too, a warm crescent moon. 'Hi, Babs.'

'Hello.' I put out my hand. I realise I did this last time we met. 'Thanks for bringing him over.'

'Not a problem.'

'Did you want to come in? You can meet my mum.'

I show him to the kitchen where Mum is sitting, reading. 'Mum, this is the boy's dad, Mahmoud. Mahmoud, this is Wendy.'

She gets up and also shakes his hand. It feels too formal, but I don't know what else to do – we don't meet new people often.

'Anyway,' I say, 'we have stuff to do so we'll be in my room.'

I've already got a pot of tea ready to go, and I laid out a picnic set on my bedroom floor. We wanted an outdoor picnic, but it's too windy. And with the curtains open and my big windows, it's almost like we're outside.

'My dad helped me make them; they're called basbousa,' the boy says as he sits down and takes the cling wrap off the cakes. 'I wanted to bring something.'

'They look delicious.'

'Can you do magic, Babs?' the boy asks as he checks out my room. I've got some dried herbs in the window, a few crystals lying around, and a big cloth of The Moon tarot card on my wall.

'Kinda,' I say. 'Not like Mum or Iris. It … scares me a little.' I've never told anyone this before. 'I don't want to accidentally curse someone.'

'I don't know if you could do that,' the boy says. He pauses. 'Not by accident.'

'Maybe.'

We sip our tea. It's nice, being still with him. He's so quiet. Maybe he is made of space. There's no sound in space. Or I guess there might be, but we just can't hear it because there's no air. I don't know how it all works.

There's a knock on my door. 'Yes?'

Mahmoud sticks his head in. 'Bye, Habibi, I'll pick you up later.'

The boy gets up to hug his dad, then Iris appears in the hallway behind them. 'Hey!' they say, and they plonk their bag on the floor. 'I've got the book I showed you and your mum a while ago, Babs.'

Mahmoud heads off, and the boy sits back down.

We're both quiet as we watch Iris take out the book. It's huge, yellowed with age, and has an embossed gold mushroom on the cover. They put it down in front of them and start flicking through the pages.

'Wow,' I say. Something in the air is different – my ears pop. That didn't happen last time.

'Saltkin reckons it's really special.' Then they take a deep breath. 'Okay, so. Even for me this is a little weird. When I found this book, all the pages were blank. You remember, Babs? You saw them.' I nod. 'A few days ago I started to like, hum, because when I found the book it was humming, so I thought maybe it liked it? And then some pages weren't blank anymore.' They stop on a page with writing and pictures in black ink. 'So I drew the sigil on my leg.' They lift their starry-patterned skirt just high enough to show us.

'Oh my god, is that scarring?' I ask.

'Nah, it just like, appeared,' they say, pulling their skirt back down. 'And then like, this wave of protection washed over me.'

'That's so cool,' the boy says. He flicks through the book a couple of times. Every other page remains blank. 'Maybe we can try a spell to reveal more pages?'

I nod. 'There must be something.'

'I reckon we give it a go,' Iris says. 'What do we need?'

'Candles, for a start,' I say. 'Maybe some herbs. And I'll get one of Mum's books.' I hurry off to the kitchen and grab the things I need, shove them into a reusable shopping bag.

When I come back, the boy is leaning over the book. 'Maybe this can tell me how to find my name,' he says.

'I dunno if you should listen to a book about that,' Iris says.

'It'd be easier.'

'Maybe, I don't know, I think you'll find it soon,' they tell him. 'And you'll know when you do.'

'Mm.'

I place the candles equal distance around the book so they make a circle. I touch their wicks and they spring to life with my own butter-yellow light.

'I didn't know you could do that,' the boy whispers.

'She's made of fire,' Iris tells him.

'Right,' he says, then we all burst into laughter because everything seems so ridiculous.

'Okay, okay.' I open the book. 'We gotta like, cleanse ourselves or whatever. I know a little about this.' I grab the glass of water on my bedside table and dip my fingers in, spreading it over my hands. 'That'll do, you both do the same. Now, uh, it says to use blood but I don't really want to? So I got some basil – I feel like it's the meatiest herb.'

The boy snorts, but he takes some.

'We're supposed to put everything in a bowl but like, this'll be fine.' I grab the saucer from my cup and place it in front of the book. I light the basil and blow it out, smoke that smells like pizza twisting around the room. I let the ashes crumble in my hands and put them on the saucer. I tell the others to do the same. Iris adds the smoky quartz from their pocket to the pile.

Nothing happens for a bit, then the candles blow out all at once. I shriek, Iris grips their knees and digs in their nails, the boy makes himself smaller.

The book flies open to a place somewhere near the front, a double-spread of spidery writing. I don't think it's in English, but Iris is leaning in, muttering what it says.

The room goes totally dark.

'Iris,' I say, but I don't think they can hear me. They're perfectly still, radiating energy. It rustles against my skin, through my hair.

Slowly, pieces fade in: a tree, grass, birdsong, river sounds. We're in the realm, I'm almost sure.

Iris finishes reading and looks up. 'What?'

'You were reading under your breath,' the boy says. 'You've taken us somewhere.'

'We're in the realm,' I say.

Iris stands up, holding out their hands. They can feel it too, the land humming.

'Do you reckon it's safe to walk around?' the boy asks.

'I'll check.' Iris takes a deep breath and steps off the picnic blanket. They gasp. 'It's so much. Like I'm being recharged. I think it's okay.'

When I step onto the grass, I don't feel any different than I do standing at home. But the air feels familiar.

'Have you been here before?' I ask.

'Don't know. Maybe it's near the birthday party clearing? The plants seem to think so.'

'You can talk to plants?' the boy says curiously.

'Oh, yes. Um. I was born from a seed. I don't mean like sperm, I mean like, a seed in the ground.'

'Oh.' He nods. 'Righto. I was born the regular way, I guess. Don't know if I'm made of anything except flesh and bone.'

'You'll figure it out,' I say. 'We can help you, if you need.'

He just nods, solemn.

There's a path through the trees, so we take it. Iris keeps the book clutched to their chest. A stream flows next to us with a low, shimmering fog lying on top of the water. I've never seen anything like it, in all my trips to the realm.

The breeze smells like something I recognise, but I can't decipher what. It's confusing, I'm not sure where it comes from.

Everything around us is humming with life. I can see the flames coming off me, showing what I'm made of. I spread my arms out, soaking up the sun.

The forest opens up for us. The tree ferns get taller, the tree trunks get wider, the flowers get bigger. There's moss over everything, flowers of every colour.

Again it's like I'm floating in space, I can't feel anything. 'Oh.'

'What?' Iris asks.

'Is it the flowers?' the boy asks, pointing to the ones I'm looking at, dark purple.

Iris bends closer to have a look. The petals end in a fire-red. They shine in a way that reminds me of the moon roses, but like a dark sun.

'Yeah.' I try to focus on my body, how I exist in it. With it. I am my body. 'Yeah, it's the flowers.' The flames on my arms are so small now I can barely see them.

'What are they? What's wrong?' Iris asks.

I start to tremble. I am my body. I *am* my body. My feet slip on the Earth, like she could just release me into space if she wanted. I am my body.

Iris puts an arm around me, but I can barely feel them. I know I'm crying, but I can't feel it.

'Babs,' the boy says, and he puts his arms around my waist, pressing himself into me. 'It's okay, we're here.'

I can't feel anything.

Iris gasps. They let go of me and stare around. 'The trees aren't happy.'

I can't move, and Iris is so quiet I don't know if the boy heard them. I notice they have a new sigil burned onto their arm from the transport spell.

'The trees aren't happy, something's wrong,' they say, louder.

'Why?' the boy asks, letting me go to look at Iris.

Iris shakes their head. 'They won't, maybe can't, answer me? It's something cold?'

'Cold?' The warmth returns, filling me up.

'It was cold that day, between the rocks,' the boy says.

'Exactly.' I spread my feet a little, feel the way Earth now locks me to her. 'We have to get out of here.'

And then, behind Iris, it's clear to me. I gasp.

It's not something I can *see*, really, but I can feel the vacuum, the cold, the wrongness. The forest is silent.

'What is it?' the boy asks.

'Cold fae,' I say. '*Run!*'

Iris starts to, but the boy doesn't move. They grab his hand, and we're crashing through the trees. We don't follow the path, just keep running. The cold presence is close behind us – I can feel it in my feet whenever they touch the ground.

'Those flowers,' I yell to the others, not even sure if they can hear me over us crashing through the forest. 'I remember seeing them when I was with the witch.'

'What?!' Iris yells back.

'Does that mean she's nearby?' the boy says.

I can't reply to that; the thought of the witch being close is too much.

We stop when we come to the stream we were walking beside before, surreal and magical. I don't think we should touch the water – the fog looks like … I don't know.

'Can we cross it?' the boy says.

'No,' Iris and I say at the same time with the same panic.

A shiver runs up my spine and I cry out. 'They're close,' I say, feeling the tug of their vacuum.

'Are these the same things as before the birthday party?' the boy asks.

'Yes,' I say, shivering. Are these figures somehow with the witch? Does she control them?

'We have to get out of here,' I say. I feel like I'm being poisoned, the tendrils of cold sweeping up my legs, into my veins, my heart. 'Come on.'

A cold hand clamps down on my shoulder. I scream. This spooks the boy even more and he shoots off, me and Iris just managing to keep up with him.

'Can you use the book?' I ask Iris as we run. 'To get us out?'

'I don't know if the same spell will work,' they say. 'We don't have all the other stuff.'

'We can't run forever,' I reply. 'Maybe having the sigil on your body will help?'

'Please, Iris, there's gotta be something you can do,' the boy says.

We're slowing down, we can't run much further. The boy is holding a stitch in his side, Iris is red in the face. 'The basket?' they ask.

'Forget it,' I say, waving a hand. 'We just have to leave.'

'Okay.' Iris drops to their knees, their skin splitting.

Bright blood blooms. The boy cries out and kneels beside them. I do the same.

Iris lies the book flat on the ground on the right page. They use the blood from their knees to trace the sigil onto the paper. 'Hold me!' they yell out, and me and the boy each grip an arm. The sigil fades into the page.

We're back in my room.

We look at each other. We're covered in little cuts from running through the trees, and breathing too heavy, too red in the face.

'I'm sorry, Babs,' Iris says.

I close the book. 'I'll get the Dettol; we should make sure our cuts don't get infected. Your knees especially.'

Before either of them can reply, I get up and go to the bathroom. I lock the door and sit on the cold tiles, my back against the cupboard.

The witch. Vada said she was far away, but we were so close. I shiver, try to remember I am my body, we're in the world together.

I take the bandaids and Dettol back to my room, where Iris and the boy clean my cuts, bandage me up.

Chapter Fifteen
The Static Girl

Babs is half visible on the bus. When I sit beside her, she smiles at me, but then I turn my head and she's gone. I reach out for her but there's just empty space. I get out my book and then she's back. As I look at her again, she flickers like static.

'Babs?'

'Those flowers,' she says. 'I can't believe they were there. I don't think I believed it.'

'What? Is that … good?' I can't tell.

Babs starts to cry; I put an arm around her but it's hard because she keeps disappearing.

'I want to see her,' she says. 'I want this gone.'

I pat her back and she cries some more.

'Why don't we find her?' I ask.

'I don't understand why Nova wouldn't want me to know.' She's stopped crying, but she's breathing heavy and she leans on my shoulder.

'They want to protect you.'

'I don't need protecting,' she mutters.

'They're just scared. I don't think it was right for them to keep this from you in the first place. That's why Vada told you.' I shiver at the memory of the coldness. 'Maybe the witch is working with the cold fae. Or . . . maybe they work for her.'

'It could be really dangerous,' Babs says, and then she's gone completely.

I take my arm back and get out my phone. I text her, tell her to let me know if she needs anything. But she doesn't respond by the time we get to school, and I have to stop checking my phone.

Babs isn't in art class, but the boy is. We sit together, feeling the absence of her.

'Do you think she's okay?' he asks, not looking at me. He concentrates on colouring in something on his page. I don't know what it is. With him, I can never tell until it's all done.

'Not really. Do you want to go to Eaglefern after school? She'll probably be there.'

He nods. 'Sure.' He colours in some more, green again. Green seems to be his favourite.

I don't know what I'm doing with this big art project. I've taken to cutting the letters out of newspapers and sticking them all over the page, hoping maybe some thoughts will appear. So far no, but it's fun and Miranda seems to like it.

'Hey,' the boy says, 'you know how you said you'd come with me to the doctor?'

I nod, but then when I look at him he's not looking at me. 'Yes.'

'Do you reckon maybe we could go? Maybe this weekend?' He's blushing, gripping his pencil with whitened fingers.

'Sure. I'm taking the pill for my period, it's good. I end up having one every few months but it's so much better than before. If that's what it's about. You don't have to tell me.'

He glances up at me then back to his page. 'Thanks. I'll make the appointment and let you know.'

'Great.'

I watch him colour a bit more before I go back to cutting out letters and words. I find an old article about plants and use that, covering the page with seeds of ideas, but still nothing takes shape.

'How are you two going?' Miranda asks.

'I'm not sure,' the boy says. The two of them start talking about his project, and I notice Miranda never uses the name the other teachers use. She uses the right pronouns because she must've heard me or Babs using them. But never in front of the class.

While they talk, I rub my glue stick all over the letter-spattered page. I get the bottle of pearlescent-pink glitter from the stores cupboard, and I shake it onto the glue. It's a strange thing, to see the letters and the words poking out through the glitter. They still don't say anything, so it's like trying to listen to a radio through static. Glittery static.

It looks ace, but it's not what I want for this project. I try to figure out if there's something I want to keep in it, to use in another piece, but I don't know what. The glitter's nice. Maybe it's not magic enough.

'How are you going, Iris?' Miranda asks.

'I don't know.' I shrug. How do I tell her that what's on the page is the mess I feel about this piece? Hidden words – thoughts, I'm not sure what it's supposed to be.

'Bit lost?'

I nod.

'What is this?' She gestures to the glittery word page.

'Not sure.'

'You're finding words a little hard today,' she says. Her face is kind.

I nod. I don't know what else to say. There's a burning within me to make something, an urge growing under the soil, the way I did. But I don't know what it is. The leaves haven't yet poked through the surface.

'It's okay. You have a few weeks, there's plenty of time.'

'Okay.'

Miranda leaves our table and goes to check in with someone else.

'What are you planning for this project?' I ask the boy.

I realise I've talked about this with Babs but not him.

'I'm just trying to figure out what my name is,' he says. 'So, I don't know.'

'I feel like I don't know anything either. I'm trying to figure out how to tell people about how I was born from a seed.'

He stares at my glittery page for a while. 'This looks just like that. Everything's obscured and magic, and you're not sure but no one else is either. I think you can use this.'

His page is rainbows. Flowing shapes, long curls of colour.

'You'll figure it out,' I tell him. 'There are lots of names. There will be one right for you. You'll probably find it when you're least expecting it.'

He gives a small smile.

We go back to our work, and Miranda tells the class that we're all doing well. One boy snickers and nudges something to his friends, but Miranda pretends she doesn't notice. She lets us go from class a few minutes early.

In the corridor I text Babs, telling her we'll be at Eaglefern for a bit after school ends. I put my phone back in my pocket before any of the teachers see me.

The boy and I head to different classes. At lunchtime it's raining so we sit in the library, mostly in silence. I keep sitting there after the end-of-lunch bell rings, skipping maths again.

Saltkin flits in through an open window and looks at me. His face is scrunched up, sad.

'Are you disappointed in me for missing another class?' I mutter so it sounds like I'm talking to myself.

His disapproval is replaced by laughter for a moment, before he gets stern again. 'Iris, you know I don't care about that. I know what happened in the forest.'

'What happened in the forest?' Maybe he doesn't know.

'With the book. Why did you transport yourselves there? That book can be dangerous, you have to look after yourself.'

'Can't this wait until after school?' I ask quietly. 'People will notice I'm talking to no one.'

'This is *important*, Iris. Can you meet me outside?'

'It's raining, Saltkin, that'll look even weirder.'

'Fine. Listen then.' He sits on my pencil case. 'You can't go looking for the witch, Iris. You made a pact with me not to. Those aren't easily broken. And you could put yourself in real danger – we don't know what she's capable of. The forest is changing.'

'It's not like you did that pact on purpose.' I can't look him in the eyes.

Red flashes across his skin, sparking out at his hands and feet. 'It doesn't matter. You have to be careful with magic, you could hurt yourself. You could hurt your friends.'

That gets me. 'You're right. But we went there accidentally, and we thought it would be fine. It looked just like where we had the party. And we weren't looking for the witch, by the way – that was a coincidence. I didn't even know what the flowers meant.'

He gazes at me for a long time, and I don't know what he's thinking. When he opens his mouth I expect him to say something, but then he shakes his head and flits right back out the window. I sigh angrily and roll my eyes. It's not like we meant to get in any danger. Everything was an accident.

I wish he had a phone.

I start working on my art project again, cutting out letters and sticking them onto the next page. I join them with a black fineliner, not in any order, just trying to make some kind of connection. I create a nonsense word, a sentence, and then I put the pen down.

I check my phone. Babs still hasn't replied.

Are you okay? I text. I wait about half a minute before writing another one. *sorry i dont mean to bug you im just worried please lmk youre okay.* I hover over send for a second, wondering if it makes me too needy or whatever, and then press it.

There's still no reply by the time the end-of-school bell goes. Me and the boy walk down the hill together, all the way to Eaglefern.

Bec is working today. I blush as I order a hot chocolate, and the boy can't look at her. 'Do we all have crushes on her?' I ask him as we start to walk over to Babs, who's sitting in her usual spot at the back. She's flickering again; I frown.

His blush grows like fairy floss. 'Maybe.'

'I do. Babs definitely does.'

'Bec's just really nice.'

'Hey,' I say, sitting opposite Babs. The boy sits next to her. 'Did you order?'

'Bec couldn't see me,' Babs says, voice barely above a whisper. 'I didn't know what to do so I just sat here. I thought Livia would be working – she normally works Mondays. I didn't want to go home because I didn't want to have to tell Mum why I was back so early.'

'Have you eaten?' the boy asks.

Bec brings over our drinks.

'Can we get a cappuccino as well, please?' the boy asks, still blushing. I didn't know he could get more red.

Once Bec leaves, Babs nods. 'I had my lunch I brought from home.'

'Do you want more?'

She shrugs, and she flickers again.

The boy looks at me.

'Why don't you come over tonight, Babs?' I ask. 'You too,' I add, looking at the boy, 'if you want. It'll be nice. I'm sure Clover and Moss won't mind.'

Bec brings over the cappuccino before anyone can reply. 'Hey, Babs, Livia says you're getting free coffee today, and we've got some focaccias I'm heating up for youse, otherwise I gotta throw them out.' She pauses, like she's noticed the way Babs looks so lost and so small. 'It's good you have each other. Make sure you stick together, okay?' She goes back to tend to the focaccias.

'I'd like that,' Babs says to me. 'Do we need to bring anything?'

'We'll manage,' I say.

Clover and Moss leave us to our own devices. Bec gave us heaps of focaccias so we have them for dinner. My favourite is the one with the pesto and sundried tomato. Babs is flickering less, and she puts extra cheese on the focaccia she's eating. It's dribbled out onto her top, but she doesn't mind.

We're in the lounge in the dark, watching an Elvis movie. It's one of the ones where he's a racing-car driver, and we're not really paying attention, though the boy sings along to every song.

'Saltkin came and saw me today in the library,' I say. 'He warned me not to look for the witch. He said it's dangerous.'

'Of course it's dangerous,' Babs says. 'I know it's dangerous.'

'The other thing is ...' I hesitate. I should have told

them earlier. 'I'm in a faerie pact to not go looking for her.'

Babs stares at me. 'What? That's so dangerous!'

'Saltkin made it with me accidentally … I should have said something sooner.' My face burns with shame.

'Iris, that's so scary.'

'What happens if you break it?' the boy asks.

'Dunno,' Babs says. 'But whatever it is, it's not good. Iris, what if *I* want to go? Without you?'

I swallow. 'I'll help you as much as I can. But Saltkin said it would be bad if I broke the pact.'

'Maybe there's a way around it.' The TV is lighting up the boy's face.

'If he's warning me, it's going to be really bad.' I turn to Babs. She's flickering, almost as much as this morning. 'Babs, come on, the boy's right. We'll figure out a way around it. Faeries are masters at words, there will be a loophole.'

Her eyes are full of tears.

'Don't worry,' I say. 'We'll be okay. We can find her.'

Chapter Sixteen
The Story of Babs and the Heavy Day

Babs was not feeling good that morning. In fact, she felt like a puddle of goo. She didn't press the snooze on her alarm, she just turned it off. Sadie huffed her big old dog lungs and kept on sleeping. A few minutes later, Wendy tapped on the bedroom door. 'Babs? Time for school.'

Babs kept her eyes closed. She didn't know how to say what she was feeling. It was like sad, but it was much more empty than that. She had always told herself that because her mother had depression, she couldn't have it. For some reason this seemed to make sense.

She rolled over to face the wall and opened her eyes. The curtains were not drawn, so she stared out of the window at the bright day. The trees that hid her house from the road swayed in the breeze. Another blustery Melbourne spring day. She usually loved them, but today she couldn't quite muster up much of any feeling.

Wendy came back and opened the door this time after knocking. 'Sweets?'

Babs looked at her, and Wendy's face softened. Although it was always soft.

Wendy sat on the bed. She put her hand on Babs's head. 'Maybe we should go see someone today.'

Babs knew she meant a GP.

'I don't think I can.'

'I'll do all the talking.' She stroked Babs's hair. 'I've been thinking this for a while.'

Babs wished she could just magic this away.

'I think most of this is from thinking about the witch,' Babs said. But she wasn't so sure. Had she always felt this yawning pit in her?

'That's probably true,' Wendy said. 'Either way, you're under a lot of stress. I'll call the doctor and see if she has any appointments available today, okay?'

Babs nodded.

Wendy left the room, and Babs listened to her talk on the phone in the kitchen. She wondered what Wendy was saying.

On the bedside table, Babs's phone vibrated with a message. She knew before checking that it would be from Iris. She told them she wouldn't be at school that day, and then she couldn't look at her phone anymore. But she couldn't put it down either, so she just lay there playing a game, matching shapes and colours.

Wendy came in to tell her when the doctor's

appointment would be that day, then left Babs to herself. She went back to sleep.

When Babs woke, her mouth was dry and her stomach was spiking with hunger. She got up, went to the toilet, and got in the shower. It was a little cold, but she couldn't quite make her hand reach the tap to change it. So she stood there, in the almost-warm-enough water, for a bit too long.

As she turned the tap off, she started to shiver. She looked in the mirror and saw her hair dye was fading. She got back into her pyjamas and sat at the kitchen table, ate some jam toast that had no flavour.

'Do you want to see the witch?' Wendy asked. 'I assumed you wouldn't want to. But maybe that's not the right thing. Do you want to try to get her to lift the curse?'

'I don't know.'

Both outcomes were bad. If Babs continued on like this, flickering in and out of life. If she met the witch and somehow got the curse lifted, she would be seen all the time. Sometimes she liked this life. She liked it a lot. It meant she could go to the realm whenever she wanted; she didn't have to go to school all the time. She could stay at home and not get into trouble.

But then Iris was the first person to see her more than once, apart from Wendy and Livia. What a lonely life. Babs imagined it stretching out across the years.

'I don't know,' Babs repeated.

'That's okay. I've got to do some work, but let me know if you need anything. Do you want to camp out in the lounge today?'

Babs wanted to stay in her room all day. 'Yes.'

Wendy got a blanket and a pillow, propped them on the couch. She shooed Babs away to the lounge while she made her some tea. Babs flicked through the app on her phone, but she didn't know what to watch. When Wendy brought out a little tray with tea, biscuits and a cupcake, she asked if Babs minded if Wendy chose what to watch. Babs shook her head. So Wendy put on a DVD of one of Babs's favourite movies from when she was a kid. Babs fell asleep on the couch halfway through. When she woke, she felt a little more alive.

When Wendy took her to the doctor, she sat in the car and stared out the window at all the trees rushing past. The witch was somewhere out there, and that was all Babs could think about as she gazed at the greenery.

After they were out of the trees, and in town, Babs felt more exposed. The witch was in the forest, yes, but the town was something else. Babs knew the forest, but the town was full of strange things. Anything could happen.

They drove through a few more towns, as the good doctor didn't live near them. When Wendy finally pulled up in front of the building, Babs wished she could sink into the seat.

'We won't be long,' said Wendy. 'And this is the hardest bit. Then it'll get easier.'

'Easier to what?'

'Know when you need help.'

Wendy led Babs up the ramp to the offices, and checked in with the receptionist. Babs stared at the stack of old magazines on the table in front of her. There were old picture books too, falling apart from so many hands.

The doctor called out her name ten minutes later and Babs followed Wendy into the room. Everything was varying shades of blue, except for the jellybeans in a jar on the desk. Dr Cheng had been seeing Wendy for a long time, but Babs had always been to the local clinic that was bulk-billed and closer to home.

Dr Cheng and Wendy talked for a while, Wendy thanking her for seeing Babs today. Wendy asked Babs a lot of questions that felt terrible to answer, but more terrible not to answer. When the questioning was done, Dr Cheng said Babs should see a counsellor. Babs stared at her hands and tried to stop the tears that were welling up. She did stop them, but there was a deep ache in her.

Dr Cheng recommended a few places and made Babs a mental health-care plan, so that if they did have to pay it would be a little cheaper. The doctor printed out a list of trans-friendly counsellors and psychologists.

Babs felt guilty that she needed something that cost money.

When they were finished, Dr Cheng gave Babs and Wendy a jellybean each.

'You can see the counsellor at school if you want,' Wendy said. 'Or we can try some of these.'

'How am I supposed to talk to someone about the witch if they'll think I'm making it all up?'

'That's a good point, Babsy. I don't know. We can think of a plan later.'

'I don't want to see the one at school.'

'Okay. We'll find someone else. I'll call around.'

Babs nodded.

When they were almost in town, Wendy asked if Babs wanted to go to the Eaglefern Cafe.

'Don't you have to do work today?' Babs asked, but she wanted to say yes. She could picture the cakes and the tarts that Livia would have baked fresh that morning.

'We won't stay long,' Wendy said.

Babs knew that meant they would probably stay for a while and then go to the op shop a few doors down.

When the doorbell tinkled as they walked in, Livia gasped. 'My two favourite girls. How are ya?' She hugged Wendy, but she could sense Babs didn't want a hug that day.

Babs said hello, then went and sat at the big cushy

couch at the back next to the window. She wished Iris and the boy were there, and the three of them were just sitting together, reading. Her friends wouldn't ask about her day, and she wouldn't have to talk about the witch.

Instead of messaging them, she looked out the window. The bees were gathering their pollen, and a faerie was sitting under the leaves of a dahlia.

The faerie was preening their wings, the way an insect does except with their fingers. Babs watched as they moved the gossamer wings through their hands. Babs had never seen a faerie do this before. Once the faerie had finished, they lay on their stomach and spread their wings out under the sun. Babs smiled.

Wendy was still talking to Livia, too softly for Babs to hear anything they were saying. She wondered if perhaps they were talking about her, or just catching up. Maybe a bit of both. Babs knew depression was nothing to be ashamed of, Wendy had had it for as long as Babs could remember. Babs knew it was a disease.

But Babs still felt shame.

Livia brought Babs a brownie. It was soft and fresh, and Babs leaned into the back of the couch as she ate it. The sun moved across the room, and Babs liked the feel of it on her skin. Just like the faerie, she bathed in the light. Babs felt like she should be doing something, like reading or messaging someone, or playing a game, but she did none of those things. She just sat there, the taste of the brownie still on her tongue, and she relished being in the sun.

Afterwards, Wendy bought a couple of things from the op shop, and they went home. Wendy went to the kitchen to do some spellwork, and Babs went to her room. She dug around in her schoolbag and pulled out the sheet for a science project due next week: a poster about an aspect of Antarctica. Babs had studied Antarctica a few times over the years, so she decided to write about the penguins with the little yellow bits coming off their faces.

She was almost half done when she realised the deep pit of her wasn't as yawning anymore. She felt lighter, less like goo. She *felt*.

So she stopped working and went out into the kitchen where Wendy was putting the finishing touches on a spell.

'I'll make dinner tonight,' Babs said. She smiled at Wendy, who smiled back.

'Thanks, Babsy.'

'Thanks, Mum. For today.'

Wendy pulled her into a hug. 'I know it's hard. But you'll be okay.'

Babs hugged Wendy with all the strength she had. 'I know.'

Chapter Seventeen
The New Scar

It's warmer than I expected on the bus ride home, the outside world moving by in dark blues and orange streetlights. The sound that passing cars make means it's been raining recently, but it's not now. The sky is stormy and thick, indigoes and greys and black. I wonder if it'll rain again. The air coming through the bus window is warm, I can taste the rain on it.

I trace the newest sigil scar on my arm. I've managed to hide it for a few days, though it's pretty and I want to show it off. Like a little flower almost, curving petals around a centre. The one on my leg is like a twig. I wonder if they're about plants because the book knows, or if it's all a coincidence.

When I get off the bus, the outside light is on, peeking through the wisteria branches. Inside, the house smells like pancakes; usually Clover only makes them in the morning, but maybe they're for dessert. When I walk into the kitchen, she hasn't noticed I'm home. She's got her daggy trackie daks on, with the dirt stains that just won't come off no matter how hard she tries, and a plaid shirt rolled up at the elbows, her hair in a bun that has half come loose. She's scrubbing something off a tray using steel wool. The pancakes must be gone already. She gives up on the tray and lets it sink into the water.

When she turns around, she jumps in fright. 'Sprout! I didn't hear you come in.'

'I just got here.'

'How was Babs's? How's her mum?'

'Yeah, they're good, it was nice.' I reach for an apple on the table, and Clover cries out.

'What is that?' she asks, pointing to my arm.

'An apple?' I ask, looking down at it. And then I notice the sigil scar, still red and raised against my skin although it's been a few days. 'Oh.'

Moss comes into the kitchen, a book she must've been reading still in her hand. 'What's wrong?'

Clover's looking at me like her heart has broken, and I wonder if there's any way I can *not* tell her about the magic.

'I didn't do it,' I say.

'What happened?' Clover reaches for Moss's hand. 'Um.'

Saltkin flits in through the open window. He looks from the scar, to my mothers, to me. A red wave travels along his skin, turns his wings into flames briefly. The kitchen feels cold.

He comes over. 'It's okay, Iris,' he says. 'Maybe you should tell them.'

I don't reply with words, but I nod.

'I'll show you,' I say to my mothers. My heart picks up, beating a little too fast. I can feel it in my throat, and I take a deep breath. The book is lighter than I remember as I take it out of my schoolbag and put it on the table.

Moss and Clover look at it, then each other.

'The book gave me the scar.' I flick through the pages until the ones that appeared at Babs's house are there.

'What does this mean, Iris?' Moss asks, sadness spilling from her words. She puts her book down on the table without marking her page. 'You got the idea from this?'

'Is this a spell?' Clover asks.

I nod. 'I can do magic. Er, like proper magic.'

'You can?' Moss asks while she watches Clover pore over the page.

'Can you read this?' Clover points towards the book.

I frown, take a closer look. I can, but now I realise it's not in English. 'I can't explain it, but yes. It's a long story.'

Clover sits down at the table, gestures for us to do the same. 'We've got time.'

I sit opposite them both, and it reminds me of times I got in trouble when I was little. But their faces are kind, and sad, and I don't want them to think this is anything other than what it is. I know they'll believe me, but still, revealing everything is strange. I've known about magic forever; I met Saltkin when I was a toddler. Back then I told my mothers about Saltkin and the other fae, and the dryads, and learning that I could talk to plants, but that was when I was small. I haven't mentioned it as if it were real in a long time.

Surely if you grow a baby from a seed in the ground, you're predisposed to believe in magic.

'Um.' I take a breath, fluttering and deep. 'Do you remember Saltkin?'

Moss nods. 'Your imaginary friend when you were little. You loved going on adventures in the backyard – you'd tell us the most wonderful stories.'

Saltkin flits over and sits in front of me on the table. They'll never be able to see him if they can't already. He gazes up at me and nods.

Clover looks at me like she knows what I'm going to say. She probably just wants the scars to be anything but what she thinks they are.

'He's real,' I say. 'And everything else I told you. All of it. Everything happened. They love your garden, Clover. And the plants tell me how much they love you.'

She blushes deep, but I can tell Moss isn't sure how to react. She watches Clover.

'So this has been going on the whole time?' Clover says. 'No wonder you would always know how to look after the plants without me ever telling you anything.'

Moss nods and looks thoughtful. 'Sometimes I would see you outside – I thought you were talking to yourself.'

'And you love to go into the forest. I always knew you'd be safe, somehow.'

'So you,' I play with my ear, not sure what to do with my hands or where to look, 'so you believe me?'

'Of course we do,' Clover says, and a weight drops off me. I knew they would, but somehow I thought that perhaps they wouldn't. 'So tell us more about this magic book.'

'Saltkin always said I wouldn't be able to do much magic, and this book has changed that. It's got lots of spells in it, but the pages have to be revealed. I've –'

'Where did the book come from?' Moss asks. 'It's not dangerous, is it?'

'I found it in a box at the op shop in town.' It might be dangerous, but I don't want to tell them that.

'It was just there?' Moss asks.

'I think it made sure I was nearby. Somehow. It was humming, I could hear it from where I was standing.'

'And how does the scar come into everything?' Moss says.

'I was reading these words out loud when the sigil appeared on the page. And then when the spell was done, it appeared on my skin.'

'This one looks different, though,' Moss says. 'It's like a stick. That one on your arm looks like a flower almost.'

'Oh.' I briefly wonder if I could lie, just tell them it was like that. But I decide to trust them, since they haven't let me down yet. 'There's another one.'

'How many in total?' Clover asks, face creasing up with worry.

'Just two,' I say.

'Well, there's a whole book here,' she says, flicking through it. 'Does this mean you'll have this many scars?'

Moss puts a hand on Clover's arm.

'I don't know if they're all sigils.' I show them the twig on my thigh. 'See, this one's a lot more faded already. I don't think they're going to be too obtrusive.'

'Do they hurt?' Clover asks.

'When they came up they smarted a bit, but not really.'

Saltkin flitters his wings. 'Can you tell Clover thank you for the garden?'

'Er, also, Saltkin is here at the moment.'

They both look around the room.

'How big is he?' Clover asks.

'Can we see him?' Moss asks at the same time.

'No, if you could you would see him already. He's small, a bit bigger than a sparrow. Maybe a mudlark. He says thank you for the garden, Clover. It's home to a lot of his friends. They love it. He says no one else could take better care of it.'

'Thanks,' Saltkin says to me, pleased by my additions.

Clover blushes rose-red. 'He's very welcome.' She's quite flustered as she puts on the kettle. 'This is all a lot to take in,' she says, laughing. 'They're all out there, are they?' She looks through the window while the kettle starts to boil.

'Iris, you didn't answer one of my questions. This

isn't dangerous, is it?' Moss asks again, tapping the book.

It could be, but I don't want to tell them. I lock eyes with Saltkin, and he knows I'm not going to say everything, but I don't see any judgement in his expression. 'No,' I say.

At lunch the next day, the boy brings his stick-and-poke gear from his locker. We sit behind one of the portables where there are lots of cigarette butts on the ground. People don't smoke as much as they used to, back when my mothers were kids, but when they do they go behind the gym because that part has cover if it's raining.

The sky is full with the promise of rain but I don't think it will fall. So no one should interrupt us.

'We gotta make sure everything is clean,' the boy says, laying down a little clear plastic sheet. He puts on some gloves, wipes something astringent on my arm to sterilise it.

'Good place to do it then,' Babs says with a smile and raised eyebrow, gesturing to the cigarette butts.

'That's a good point,' he says. 'Like, I've done it to myself in places like this, but I don't know if I should do it here.'

'It'll be fine, right?' I ask.

'The tattoo is basically an open wound when it's done, so I dunno if this is right. I'd feel awful if it got infected, if I got you sick.'

'Hm.' My desire to have something pricked into my skin forever is overwhelming. I love the rose on the back of his arm. I'm going to get a moon rose on my shoulder, so it's hidden by the sleeve of my uniform.

'We could go somewhere,' Babs says. 'Like ... somewhere.' At this she waggles her eyebrows up and down.

That could be ace, but I wonder if we'll accidentally find the witch flowers again. 'I don't know, it could be dangerous.'

'We could just like, go to my house,' says the boy. 'No one's home.' He pauses for a moment, packing everything back into the bag. 'Well, no one except Lunchbox.'

'D'you need the book to do the spell?' Babs asks. She's drawn up a geometric pattern she wants on her thigh, but that will take more than a lunchtime to do.

'I'm not sure.' I run my fingers over the scar flower. 'Let's try.' Each of them takes one of my hands, and I close my eyes and picture the sigil.

When I open my eyes, I see my feet still surrounded by cigarette butts.

'Maybe not?' I say.

'One more time?' Babs says. She squeezes my hand. 'I reckon you can do it.'

'Okay.' I close my eyes again. I can't remember the words on the page of the book, but I trace the sigil in my mind and think about the boy's house. The deck, where we dyed his hair. There was rain, there might be rain today. I concentrate on the feeling of Babs's and the boy's hands in mine.

When I open my eyes it's raining, and we're on the deck, safe and dry. Lunchbox looks over from where he's curled up on a chair, then goes back to sleep.

'Holy shit!' Babs says, letting go of my hand to jump up and down. 'You did it!'

'That's so cool,' the boy says before starting to set up his tools. 'This is much safer.' He puts gloves on, wipes my skin down again to make sure it's clean, and then unwraps a needle from a packet. He squeezes out some ink into a little container and then dips in the needle. 'If you want me to stop, tell me,' he says. 'And just relax – it'll hurt, but it's like a cat scratch. Not too bad.' He takes my arm in a gloved hand, and I'm surprised by the warmth of his fingers. He's holding my arm gently but firmly, so I don't move with the needle. The first prick startles me, but I tell him to keep going. It's strange, thinking about how this is going to be on my skin forever.

I wonder what Clover and Moss will say when they find out. I think they'll appreciate it – he's a good artist – but they'll say I'm too young. It's not like I'm getting something ugly. It's a flower; it's *my* flower, from our garden. And after the larger revelation about magic, maybe my mothers can handle this.

I feel the needle pricking in a curve, and I wonder

which bit of the flower he's doing. He showed me the sketch but he does everything freehand on the skin. I wonder how many other people he's done this to. He clears his throat and shifts a bit; I realise how close he is. I slow my breathing, matching it to his. Closing my eyes, I feel the needle go in and out, quick, brief, it doesn't really hurt at all. At times he adjusts his hold on my arm, always making sure the skin isn't too tight. 'How are you going?' he asks.

I open my eyes, and he's even closer than I thought. 'It's fine,' I say, for the first time noticing just how long his eyelashes are.

When he lets go of my arm, I miss the warmth of him. He takes a photo on his phone and shows me. 'What do you think?'

It's perfect, the thin outline of one of my moon roses. The skin around the lines is slightly red, but I was expecting more. More pain. 'I love it,' I say. I want to touch it, feel the lines that will be there forever.

'I have to go over it a couple more times, just to make sure it'll look good. Need a break?'

I shake my head. 'It doesn't hurt.'

Babs is reading in a seat in the corner. She's got a cup of tea in one hand, the steam curling up to the deck's plastic roof while the rain falls nearby, not touching her.

'Maybe some tea, though,' I say. 'Do you want one?'

He smiles, small and certain. 'Sure.'

In the kitchen I boil the kettle and catch myself going

to touch the tattoo too many times, so I put my hands flat on the bench until the kettle flicks off. I choose two cute matching teacups with a delicate floral pattern, make the tea, watch the milk swirl around like a storm. I stir seven times clockwise, trying to put some goodwill into the liquid. I think it shimmers a bit, but it's so fleeting I don't know.

When I sit back down on the deck, I hear the boy sip his tea and sigh, maybe a little more content than he normally would be. 'Ready?' he asks, loading the needle with some ink.

'Ready.'

I could almost fall asleep to it, the rhythm of the needle. The sound of the rain. The quiet contentment of Babs, the hush of the boy's breathing, so close.

When he's done, I don't want it to be over. He pats the tattoo down with an alcohol wipe, smears a cream on it, and then puts cling wrap around my arm. It's high enough that my shirt can cover it, but I put my jumper back on anyway.

The boy says it will take about two weeks for the lines to heal, and I have to buy a special cream at the supermarket to put on it. 'Babs, we'll do you next week,' he tells her. 'Should we go back to school? Lunch is over soon.'

Babs and the boy hold my hands again. They finally get me up after four tries. I don't really want to return. We have to split up to go to our classes. Through my last period of the day, maths, I can feel the moon rose on my skin, not because it's painful but because it was put there by the boy. I run a hand through the hair on my head, cut by Babs.

That night while I'm going to sleep, I look out the window and see a few stars peeking between clouds.

Saltkin flits into the room and sees the rose, sparkly peach clouds bursting in the air around him. 'I thought you said you were too young!' he says, hovering above the skin. 'It's lovely, Iris. Very powerful.'

'Powerful?'

'It's been infused with a lot of friendship, a lot of love. He must've been thinking about that when he was doing it.'

I crane my neck to get a glimpse. It looks like it's glowing a little under the moonlight, just like the moon roses.

Chapter Eighteen
The Rose Tattoo

I think remembering that me and my body are the same thing is helping, because the teachers keep telling 'us three' to stop talking and do some work. Art class is the worst for me still, which is a shame because Miranda is the best teacher.

I draw the witch flowers. I put on my headphones and listen to the song I was going to do my art project on, the one with the swooping electric noise and the crystal voice of a girl. The flowers aren't always purple and red, sometimes just greylead, sometimes in spidery fineliner, sometimes gone over with watercolours in blue and purple and green, aliens sprouting through the page.

Iris and the boy can't see me, though I'm sitting at their table. They're talking about the project and I want to say something, but I can't. I leave my headphones on and draw flowers.

I spend the rest of the day in the library, just drawing the flowers, going over and over the lines.

When it's time to get the bus to go to the boy's house, I still feel like I'm clouded in fog, but I run to the stop and make it just in time. The others see me, and I breathe a sigh.

Mahmoud is in the kitchen; he waves when he sees us. 'Does anyone want anything?' he asks after gathering the boy into a big hug.

'Thanks, Dad, but it's okay, we're going to go upstairs,' the boy says all in one breath and basically pushes us up the steps.

Me and Iris haven't seen his room yet. I don't know what to expect – I've never been in a boy's room before.

'Your dad's really nice,' I say as we climb the stairs.

'Yeah, he's good.' The boy smiles when we reach the landing. 'Ready for your rose?'

At first I wanted something else, then I thought I should probably get one matching Iris's and the boy's. It's going to be on my thigh. High enough that my school dress will hide it, though other dresses and skirts will show it. I don't think Mum will be mad.

When the boy opens his bedroom door, warmth floods out. He's got a desk with two big computer monitors on it, his bed is messy with dark sheets, and he has lots of books on his shelves. I go over and look at some of the spines – they're sci-fi and fantasy. 'I didn't know you read so much.'

He blushes. 'Kids at my old school teased me for it.'

'Have you read all these books?' Iris asks. There's

so many, all well-worn like they've been read heaps of times.

He nods.

'Maybe next time can you put an alien head on me?' I point to the LET'S BE FRIENDS patch on my jacket. 'That'd be rad.'

'Oh!' says the boy. 'Sure.'

'You should get a spaceship,' I tell him, and he smiles. I got a new patch the other day, MY GIRLFRIEND IS THE MOON, and it's got a crescent moon on it. It's covered in glitter.

His bed is a double, and we sit on top while he gets out the stick-and-poke things. He hands me the razor, and I start shaving the patch of skin that'll get the rose on it. I don't shave my legs a lot, and as I run my fingers over the hairless skin, it's so soft I think I might do it a bit more sometimes.

I watch as the boy sanitises everything, then a look of absolute concentration comes over his face, the point of his tongue sticking out between his teeth.

'I've been thinking about how to get around my pact with Saltkin,' Iris says as I stare at the needle. 'But I still don't know. I can't go looking for the witch, that's what I promised.'

'There must be something else,' I say. *There has to be*. 'A way you can be safe but still come with us.'

'Maybe if you just … follow us,' the boy says to Iris. 'If we go, and you don't come with us straight away. But then you follow after a bit.'

Iris frowns. 'I wonder if that would work?'

'You could ask Vada or Nova,' I say.

'Ready?' the boy asks me. I nod.

Then I wince. I knew it would hurt – it's just like the boy said, like a cat scratch.

'Sorry,' the boy says. 'You okay?'

'Yeah, all good.'

He slowly dots out the flower, not the witch's rose but our own. Like Iris's moon rose, like the boy's original rose. No more witch flowers. I decide not to draw them anymore.

Soon the dots start to look like an actual rose, soft petals curling over each other. I lean against the wall, and we all sit in silence while the first outline is done. 'How's that?' the boy asks as he wipes away extra ink with a cool wet cloth.

'Looks good.' The outline is perfect, exactly how I wanted it to be. 'Hey, look – it's in the same place as your sigil, Iris.'

'You should get your spaceship there,' they tell the boy.

'That would be cool.' He smiles. 'But Babs, what are we going to do about your witch?'

I sigh. 'I don't know. Supposing there's a way around the pact, I reckon we should just set out. Leave notes for our parents? I don't know how long this will take.'

'We should bring supplies, food and stuff.' Iris traces

something through their skirt. 'My protection sigil should come in handy. And I'll see if I can find Vada tomorrow after school – maybe they can help in some way.' Iris sighs. 'I wish I could ask Saltkin.'

The boy finishes cleaning, then dips the needle in the ink. 'Does anyone want a tea before we start again?'

'I'll make it,' Iris says, and they go downstairs.

'They're pretty upset,' the boy says as he starts to prick the rose again.

'I would be, too.'

Blood dots my skin and the boy wipes it away, quick as it came. 'We'll figure something out.'

A few minutes later, Iris comes up with a tray. They make us all tea while the boy keeps going with the rose. I take a sip of mine, just the right temperature. Perfect. And the rest of the night is the same. Once my tattoo's finished and wrapped up, we sit on the boy's bed and read some of his sci-fi books. I've got one about a giant bear, all about taking care of a strange creature. We sit like this till it's time to sleep, and we curl up in his bed.

Today the forest is bursting with bellbirds, pinging through the trees. I didn't tell Mum I was going into the national park; she was sleeping when I left. I'm in my school dress, and I was planning on going to school – but then, well, I hadn't seen the trees in so long. And maybe I can find Vada or Nova and ask them about Iris's bond.

My fingers brush against a fern, and the forest is still. Not calm, just still. The witch is here. She's not close, she's far away, but yeah. She's in the forest.

'Nova?' I say out loud. Will they come? I keep walking the path, and I pass a couple of bushwalkers in hats and Aerogard. Once they're gone, I touch the nearest tree trunk before stepping off the path.

The wind picks up, carrying coldness. Cold fae. The edges of the forest are teeming with them. I shiver. I don't reckon they're too close. I close my eyes, breathing steady so my heart calms down. I try to listen to the bellbirds. But my heart still booms in my ears.

Nothing's working, but I keep walking. The cold fae are close, I can feel them closing in around me. On all sides. I hold the heart-shaped rose quartz on my necklace, imagine love. Feel love. Iris and the boy. There's cool breath on me, wisping around my ankles as I walk, blocking out the sun, but the fae don't touch me.

'Babs?'

As I hear Vada's voice, the cold fae dissipate.

'*What* are you doing?' Their voice is stern. There's a vine growing around them and it's flowering, the tiny blooms sprouting on top of their head and shoulders. Some bees are harvesting pollen.

'I was looking for you or Nova.'

'It's not safe!' Vada frowns. 'What are you doing here at a time like this?'

'I have to ask you about something.' I swallow.

I wonder if Vada will tell Saltkin what I say, but there's no one else to ask. 'It's about faerie bonds.'

Vada runs their eyes over my face. 'What about them?'

'I just wanted to know if there are ways around them.'

'What did you promise?'

'I didn't. Iris promised Saltkin they wouldn't look for the witch.'

'Oh, Babs. We just want you all to be safe.'

I roll my eyes. 'Everyone keeps saying that. I don't need protecting! I can fight.'

'It's dangerous.'

'*I know.*' What else can I say?

'What was the specific wording of the pact?'

'That they wouldn't go looking for anything dangerous. Wasn't specifically the witch.'

Vada's sigh sounds like the wind through millions of leaves. 'Well, I suppose your friends could follow you. You look for the witch, they look for you.'

'Do you think that would work?'

Vada stares at me for ages, the seconds stretching out between us. 'If they don't help you on your journey, that should satisfy the bond.'

'Okay. Thanks.' I sigh in relief.

'Though if Iris talks to Saltkin about it, he may release the bond.'

'He won't.'

Vada shakes their head sadly. 'If that's what Iris thinks. When are you setting off?'

'I don't know. Soon.'

'Three humans in the forest alone, looking for the witch – you have to be very careful.'

'I know.'

We say goodbye, and Vada walks away. The wind picks up, almost blowing me over. The trees are wild, their limbs liquid as they sway back and forth. It's like they're made of rippling muscles.

Crack. A branch crashes into the undergrowth, its sound echoing. I have to get out. I run back to the path. As soon as I step onto it, the wind almost totally dies down.

The rose quartz hums softly.

Chapter Nineteen
The Blank Potential

My sketchpad is almost empty, its thick white pages stark. All of a sudden, I don't know how anyone can do anything. I flick to the pages before, where I wrote all that stuff about being in the ground, the page of glitter. It isn't nearly enough.

We're in art class. The boy has scribbles covering his page, and as I'm watching he flicks to the next one and draws balloons again; these ones are all different shades of green.

'How are you doing that?' I ask him.

'You're thinking about it too much,' he replies. I watch him colour a bright grass-green balloon. 'Have you heard from Babs today?' he asks.

I shake my head. 'But I'll text her at recess.'

'I hope she's okay. I haven't seen her at all. Hang on.' He goes to the supplies cupboard and returns with green pencils in shades that he hasn't used. And in front of me he plops glitter, glue and a set of watercolours. 'Do something with these,' he says.

'Do what?'

'Don't think about it, Iris.' When I scowl, he smiles and shakes his head. 'All right, fine – draw a moon rose.'

I stare at my page, large and wide and white. Maybe not empty, but full of potential. Like winter.

Miranda has lots of books around the classroom, on flowers and animals and anything else we might want to draw. So I grab one, and I try to find the moon roses. When I don't see them, I pick the fattest rose I can find and start to copy it in greylead. It's not quite right, but not bad for a first go, and the watercolours are easy enough to use on the background and the leaves. I just don't know how to colour a shining pearl-white rose.

Miranda eventually makes her way to me, while I'm starting to put glitter on the leaves and the moss below. The rose is still a greylead outline.

'How are you going, Iris? This looks wonderful.'

'I don't know how to do the rose,' I say. 'It's white. How do you colour *white*?'

'Hm.' Miranda gets out the book with all the flowers. 'Look at this one – it's white, but see, the shadows are blue. And it's got some yellows, near the centre. If you look closely, it's lots of different colours.' She puts her hands on the page so that only a small square of petal is showing. It's white, yeah, but pink and pale blue as well. The delicate veins run through the petals, and they're a darker white.

My phone buzzes in my pocket; Miranda pretends not to hear. 'Try using blues,' she tells me. 'They're a good place to start. Start with the palest and see how you go.'

'Okay.' I nod and pick up the paintbrush. I trace some of the outline, using mostly blues, some yellows. Even a bit of pale pink. As I let the paper dry, I glance at my phone under the table. It's Babs. I check to see where Miranda is: she's moved to the other side of the classroom. My phone on my lap, I open Babs's message.

I can feel the witch here.

My heart skips. *Where are you?* I hope she's not in the forest, or where the cold fae are.

'Hey,' I say to get the boy's attention. 'Has Babs texted you?'

He checks his phone. 'No. What's up?'

I show him the message, and we both wait for her reply. It doesn't come.

'I'll call her.' I've only ever called my mums before, I'm pretty sure, but this seems like an emergency. 'Can you let Miranda know I've gone to the toilet, if she says anything?' I ask the boy. He nods. We're supposed to get our planners signed by a teacher if we're ever out of class, but no one checks anyway, and I don't think Miranda would mind.

I keep my phone in my hand as I walk to the bathroom. I go into the stall closest to the wall and press the icon next to Babs's name. I wait for her to answer. I wait, and wait, the rings like heartbeats, too fast, too fluttering. I wish my own heart would stop being so loud, I wish my throat would open up so I could breathe again.

The rings stop, and for a second I can't hear anything. I think that it's just hung up automatically, but then I realise Babs is on the other end of the line. I can't hear her but I can hear a magpie in the background. 'Babs?'

'Iris.'

'Where are you?'

'I'm in the forest.' Her voice is vacant, like she's not paying attention to me properly, or that some of her is missing.

'Where? Are you with Nova? Is the witch nearby? The cold fae?'

'I'm just in the forest,' she says. 'The normal bit, with the walking trails.'

'You sound a little far away.'

'Sorry.'

'You said you could feel the witch.'

'Just in the air. The feel of the forest. I think the wind is trying to tell me something.'

'Can you go to Eaglefern?' I ask. I don't want her to be in any danger. 'We can meet you there. Me and the boy.'

'I don't know if you'll be able to see me.'

'That's okay. I just need to know you're safe.'

'I'm safe.'

'The forest isn't always safe.'

'You sound like one of them!'

'Can you just come to the cafe?' I ask, gripping the phone so hard it hurts my hand. 'Babs, please. I don't think it's a good idea for you to be there alone right now.'

Silence.

'Babs?'

Has she hung up? I check the screen. Still there.

'I'll see you at Eaglefern, okay?'

She sighs. 'Okay. After school?'

'I'll come now.'

Back in class, the boy notices the way I'm shaking, how I've paled. 'You okay?'

'Babs is in the forest, she says she can sense the witch.' My heart feels like it's trying to leave through my mouth. 'I told her to go to Eaglefern, I said I'd meet her there now.'

'But school is on.'

'Yeah but, I don't know. I'll figure out something.' I should have just not come back to class, asked the boy to look after my books and pencil case.

'Just say you'll go to the sick bay,' he says. 'I'll take you.'

So I ask Miranda if the boy can take me there for cramps. I look so pale and shaky that it seems like I'm telling the truth, and she lets us leave.

Once we're out of the classroom, we go get our bags and head off. No one stops us. The boy is shakier than me now, worried that we'll get in trouble. But we don't; nothing happens.

As we walk into the cafe, Livia frowns at us. 'School out early?' she asks.

'Uh,' I say as we both just stand there.

She smiles. 'I'm only having a go. English breakfast and a hot chockie?'

'Yeah, please. Is Babs here?' I ask, but even before she replies, I know the answer.

'No. Should she be?'

The boy and I exchange glances.

'What do we do?' he asks me.

'Is she okay?' Livia asks.

'We just thought she would be here. It's okay.' I tug the boy over to the couches. 'I'll call her.'

There's no answer. The boy texts her a couple of times, but she doesn't reply. We've been waiting a while, and Livia has brought over our drinks.

'What are we going to do?' the boy asks me again.

'I wish I could just like, call Saltkin. Or maybe Vada. Even Nova. Gosh, I don't know. Do you think she's okay?'

The boy is tight-lipped, and he doesn't reply.

Our phones buzz at the same time: it's Babs. In the group chat, she's just said *coming*.

I sigh, sinking into the couch. 'Okay. All right. Good.'

The boy starts to make his tea, and I watch the ritual. He spoons in half a sugar, which he normally doesn't do. He sits back with me, and after sipping the tea he sighs too. 'Good.'

We don't talk again until Babs comes in, her hair a mess. Her shirt says WHEN WILL I CHANGE. She looks like she hasn't slept, or she slept in the forest. Her hands are dirty. She sits opposite us without a word.

'Are you okay?' I ask her.

'Look, no.'

'Want a coffee?' the boy asks, and she nods.

He gets up to order, and I go sit beside Babs. I take her hand, and she leans into me, rests her head on my shoulder.

'What happened?' the boy asks when he comes back.

'Nothing,' she says. 'I just went into the forest to talk to Vada. They said if you follow, that should be okay … But it's so dangerous. What if you accidentally lead us even one step? I should go alone. I want to see her.'

'No, we can still do it together. You look for the witch, and I'll follow. Please don't go alone.'

Livia brings over the coffee; Babs sips it for a while. She starts to perk up a bit, her face less pale, the bags under her eyes less pronounced.

'We should stick together,' I press. The thought of Babs going by herself is unbearable. 'Please.' I look to the boy for some reassurance.

He smiles at Babs. 'I'm in too, if you are.'

'All right.' She nods.

That night, when Clover and Moss have gone to sleep, I turn off my light and bring the old book out from under the bed. It seems heavier than usual, and dustier. I sneeze, and then I see Saltkin at the window. A thunderstorm is brewing, I can taste it in the air.

'Hey, sprout,' Saltkin says, watching the book.

'Saltkin, Babs says she can feel the witch in the forest.'

'Babs knows a lot of things.' He flits over and sits on my bedspread, near the book. 'You be careful, Iris. I told you, magic is dangerous.'

'Yes, I *know*.' I wave a hand. 'I'm not going to look for the witch.'

His expression suggests that he knows we've found the loophole. 'So what are you doing now?' he asks, pointing to the book.

'I was going to ask for more protection. Not just for me, but for my friends too. You know, considering the witch and everything. Magic is supposed to be *dangerous*.'

'Please take this seriously,' Saltkin says, his wings flaming a little.

'I am, I am.' I open the book and run my hands over the blank pages, trying to figure out where to stop searching for the right one. I let the book guide me, I'm not sure how, but I stop at a page towards the end. It hums under my fingertips.

'That's very powerful,' Saltkin says. 'This is going to drain a lot of energy.'

I close my eyes, place a palm on each page in the spread. The book vibrates.

'Sprout, *careful!*' Saltkin says. But he sounds so far away.

I feel like I'm sinking into the bed, spongy mattress all around me. I can't feel the breeze from outside anymore; the distant rumble of thunder is gone. There's just the pressure of my hands against the book, and then everything fades, quick, sure.

When I wake, I'm sprawled over the book and my bed, out of the covers. It's raining hard, and it's so dark. My arms are asleep; it takes a couple of goes to push myself back into a sitting position. There's a dull burning over my ribs.

I lift up my top and see another sigil, more complex than the others, swirls looping in and out of each other, fine lines striking through. No wonder it took so much energy.

I wonder where Saltkin went. Thunder is rumbling through the house, through my bones, through the earth. The trees shake in the wind and lightning strikes across the sky.

He's probably in the forest again, making sure no fires start. I lie with my window open, the breeze coming in again, until I fall asleep.

The next day, the boy's nervous, trembling. The roses on his arm have multiplied. We're waiting in the doctor's office so that he can get a script for something to stop his periods. He had to give his legal name to the receptionist, but they explained that he doesn't have to use it again.

He has a form for new patients and is tapping a pen against the paper. He's filled everything in: birthdate, address, medical stuff. Except the name field.

'This sucks.' He puts down the pen.

'Hey, it's okay. You can just ask them to call you the boy.'

'That's only okay if you and Babs do it.'

On the one hand, I'm happy that me and Babs can make him happy that way, but on the other, I wish he could have some peace.

'I'm just gonna use my old name, I guess.'

'Maybe you can get them to make a note to only use your last name?'

He pauses for a moment; the frown slips off his face. 'Oh. That'd work.' He scribbles in his surname, Bahrani, and takes the form to the receptionist.

'Do you want me to come in with you?' I ask when he sits back down.

'I think I'd like to go alone.' His jaw is set, hard. 'I want to.'

'Sure.' I nod. 'I'm just glad you're here.'

'Me too.'

When he's called into the doctor's room, he gives me a little wave. They're in there for a while, but when he comes back out he's holding a script and beaming.

Later we're on a tram to the city, where we can get the train home.

I ask the boy, 'Do you know about gender euphoria?'

He shakes his head.

'I think, when you smiled after realising you could just use your last name, that might've been it.'

'Is it just like, good feelings? About gender?'

'It's like … the opposite of dysphoria.'

He stares out the window, watching the shops go past. 'I've only heard of gender dysphoria before.'

'I found out about it a while ago, but yeah. I thought I should let you know.'

He smiles, lost in thought.

Chapter Twenty
The Flower Ravine

It's close to dawn when my phone alarm goes off under my pillow. Time to go look for the witch. I shake myself out of the deep sleep buried in me, and poke the boy. 'Wake up,' I say when he blinks at me.

He groans, but he gets up.

We packed everything last night, so all we do is change into our hiking clothes. I wish I could put on some makeup, for extra courage, but it'll just be sweated off anyway. We use our phone torches to make sure we don't miss anything.

Iris stirs when I pass nearby, and I cover the torch but they're already awake.

'Hey,' I say, crouching beside them. 'We're off now. Don't forget your extra water in the fridge.'

They nod, and I can see them slipping back into sleep. 'Okay. Be safe.' They yawn and close their eyes.

'See you soon,' I say, but I don't know if they hear me.

We slip out of the room and lace up our shoes. The kitchen light's on.

'Hey, Mum.' I kiss her cheek. She's made us porridge. 'Aw, thanks.'

'And some sandwiches, please take them.' She nods to a stack of multigrain sandwiches next to her on the table. 'It's not a lot, but you shouldn't weigh yourselves down.'

'Thanks, Mum.'

I put the cream cheese, avocado and cucumber sandwiches in my bag.

'Please be safe,' she says. She grips my hand a little tighter than normal.

'We will be.'

I hug her, and the boy and I basically inhale our porridge. The plan is that if Mahmoud or Iris's parents come looking for us, we've just gone camping for the weekend. Mum's covering for us because she's the only person who gets what we're doing. Which might not be the best plan, but it's the only thing that can get me to the witch.

Mum clutches her mug of coffee. 'Send word if you need. I'm sure Iris could figure out how to.'

'We'll be okay, I promise. Don't worry too much.'

'Being a parent means constantly worrying, Babs. It's just my job.' She smiles at me.

I hope we're not gone for too long – if Mahmoud, Moss and Clover get worried it'll be bad. And it's not like Mum can tell them where we've actually gone.

'Take this, will you?' Mum says. She rustles through the mountain of stuff in the middle of the table, and eventually puts her hand in a pot. She gets out a stone and gives it to me. It's clear with shards of black inside – the tourmalinated quartz Livia gave to me to pass on to Mum. When I handed it to her, she explained that gems with other gems inside them can mean two things, or be twice as powerful. This one is a good luck charm, and it's protective. I rotate the stone in the light and feel secure in the spaces between the tourmaline. 'Thanks, Mum.'

'Just make sure you get home safe.'

'We will.'

We hug one more time, so hard I reckon my arms might fall off, then me and the boy go out the back door, through the garden, and into the trees.

It's still a little dark, though the sun is starting to rise. A magpie is singing, its voice curling around the eucalypts. A few butterflies flit through the trees.

As we walk, I realise I've never gone down this path before. It just keeps going and going to the left, next to way more foliage than I'm used to – not just the national park plants, but the ones from the realm, too. The air's thick with moisture and the smell of soil. We have to squeeze past trunks for a while. Then, as the trees ease off, the boy picks pine needles out of my hair.

The tourmalinated quartz in my pocket warms up. I swallow. It's probably fine.

'Can you feel that?' the boy asks.

I turn around and see he's shivering. It takes a sec for me to realise that because I'm holding the protection, I can't feel the chill. When I take his hand, he relaxes straight away. 'Cold fae must be nearby,' I tell him.

'How come it helps when we're holding hands?'

'The stone Mum gave me.'

'And I guess you *are* made of fire.' He grins. 'Nice one.'

I never thought of that. Maybe it's one of the reasons I've barely come across them, and I've walked through the realm heaps in my life.

We keep walking, hand in hand, for what feels like ages. My stomach rumbles, so we stop for a snack. I dig through my backpack for the muesli bars we packed last night, but they're not in here. The boy checks his. Looks like we put them in Iris's bag. 'We've got trail mix?' he asks, bringing out a bag full of nuts and dried fruit. I made sure we got the one with pineapple.

We sit eating for a while. Soon, we hear something new. I strain my ears. 'Reckon it's Iris.'

Neither of us says it might not be. We listen to the crunch of leaves underfoot, someone mumbling under their breath. Then through the trees we see a flash of red.

'Iris!' I say when I see it's definitely them.

A smile fires up in their face, and they wave. They half-jog over and gather us both in a hug. 'How was your morning?'

'We passed some cold fae, but they seemed to stay back as long as I had this stone my mum gave us.' I show Iris the quartz. They reach out to touch it, and a buzz of static electricity jolts us both. 'You get here okay?'

They nod. 'They followed me for a bit, too. But I'm okay. I made a protection sigil with the book, I think it'll come in handy with your stone.' They point to their chest.

'Hm, okay, good. But maybe the cold fae know we'll be here for a while, and there'll be plenty of opportunity to get us off guard.'

The boy swallows nervously. 'Do you really think they know stuff like that?'

'Probably. Here –' I pass him the stone. 'You should have it. Keep it in your pocket.'

'Thanks.' His fingers fold over the stone, he grips it tight. 'All right. Let's keep going.' He nods, determined.

The day is long, and Iris's and the boy's watches stop working. Well, they keep going, but they used to be synced up and now they're showing different times. We only noticed because I tried to check the time on my phone, but it wouldn't turn on.

'When I met the witch,' I say, 'time went strange. Maybe this is that?'

'Does that mean we'll be gone for longer or shorter than the time outside the realm?' Iris asks.

'Last time it was shorter, I think.' I try to remember the details. 'Yeah, it felt like I was gone for ages, but then when Mum found me I'd barely been gone at all.'

The realm feels different compared to all the times I've walked in it before. The air is closer, denser, wetter. There are insects on the ground I've never seen before, kind of like Christmas beetles but translucent.

I notice Iris tracing their protection sigil under their shirt, over and over.

We keep walking, mostly aimlessly. The cicadas are singing, and sometimes it seems we get real close to stepping on them. I almost feel like I know where I'm going, like there's a deep hidden memory of how to reach the witch.

'It doesn't feel unsafe here,' the boy says, when the sun is high in the sky. 'I thought it would be scarier.'

'Yeah,' I say, not feeling as optimistic but not wanting to bring him down. 'So far, so good. Let's stop and have lunch.'

The river is close by, so we sit on a big flat rock near it. While Iris refills our water bottles, I plate up the sandwiches, and the boy takes out the thermos of chai he's been carrying.

'Do you think we'll have to camp tonight?' Iris asks.

I nod. 'None of this seems familiar. You recognise it?'

Iris shakes their head.

'Do you think we're going in the right direction?' the boy asks.

'Yeah.' I don't know how I know, maybe a memory, but it's the right way.

As the boy pours the tea into our metal camping cups, the sun begins to set. The birds start to quieten.

'It was just like … lunchtime, right?' I ask.

The boy and Iris nod, looking around.

'We better get the tent set up before it's pitch-black.'

I zip open the bag, and it's super easy to put together. Me and the boy set it up while Iris gathers sticks for a campfire. Once it's all ready, we keep having our tea and sandwiches.

'Do you think this will be one night, or will it be like, the rest of the day and the whole night?' the boy asks.

Iris and I look at each other. I shrug. 'Dunno. Guess we have to wait and see.'

We fall into silence, and although we only got up a few hours ago, I start feeling drowsy. But I know something's out there. Can't sleep yet.

Iris seems to read my mind. 'I feel like something's there.' They touch the ground and close their eyes, frowning. Their face shifts from concern to guilt. They open their eyes, and I turn to where they're looking. It's Saltkin.

He's a deep red, and he flies right up to Iris's face. 'I *told* you not to do this!' He points a finger at them. 'I'm trying to keep you safe. We don't know what this witch can do!'

'I couldn't let Babs go on her own,' they say. They look

at me as if I could help, but I don't know what to say.

'This is a total rejection of everything I've ever taught you. How could you try to get around our bond, Iris?'

'I couldn't let her go by herself, and she would've. I *couldn't* let her. I love her so much, Saltkin.'

The campfire flares up when Iris says they love me. The fire in me burns brighter, too.

Saltkin sighs, and he fades into peach. 'I understand why you did this, Iris, but you've hurt me a lot.'

They hold out a hand for him. 'I know, I'm sorry.'

'Thank you,' he says, ignoring the hand. Then he flies past them to sit next to the fire, and stares into it.

I don't know where to look. We finish eating in silence, Iris so heavy, then the three of us fall asleep in the tent. Saltkin stays outside, keeping watch.

When I wake, it's still dark. I have no idea how long I was asleep, but I'm alone in the tent. I lie still and listen to the crickets outside, to the boy and Iris chatting next to the fire. Can't tell what they're saying. I wriggle out of my sleeping-bag and put my pants on.

When I get out there, the boy and Iris are huddled together. 'Oh good, we were just about to wake you,' the boy says.

'Why?'

A howl splits the night. Is that a wolf? I stumble a little in my rush to sit next to the others on the log.

Iris is pale. 'We're not sure what to do.' They trace the sigil through their shirt.

'Hope for the best?' I say. 'I dunno. Are there wolves in the realm?'

'What if it's something else?' the boy asks.

Saltkin flickers into view, coming back from flying in the forest. 'It's okay. I'll protect you.' He throws a handful of powder into the fire, and it flares blue before returning to its regular colour.

While the spell keeps whatever is howling away from us, we can hear its calls through the dark. They keep getting closer. One's so close I feel like I should be able to see whatever is howling, should be able to reach out and put my hands in its fur, but nothing's there.

It feels like the night goes for a few days, but we don't feel the need to eat, or go to the toilet, or even to shower. By the time a fresh dawn breaks through the trees, we're ready to go on an all-day hike. Anything to get away from the howls that haven't stopped till now.

Saltkin says he has to leave, and he kisses Iris's forehead before he goes. We wish he could stay, but he has things to take care of.

We walk for a few hours in a row, not talking much. After we stop for lunch, we come across a ravine. It's impossibly deep, and damp cold air seeps from it. We stand next to it for a while, contemplating the distance.

Then I notice something growing in the ravine. 'There they are!' I say. 'The witch flowers.' Iris gasps, the boy pats me on the arm.

I shiver. She's so close.

Do I really want to risk meeting the witch? And do I really want her to take the curse away? I frown. Of course I do.

'Well, we can't cross that,' the boy says.

'Looks like we have to, though,' I reply. I don't want to have put Iris and the boy in danger for nothing. We've come so far already.

'Maybe there's a bridge somewhere,' Iris says, 'if we walk along it for a bit. Or it'll get smaller.'

So we start to walk again, the cool air now making us all shiver. The birds aren't singing, I realise, and the witch flowers aren't growing in this part of the ravine.

'There's something in the trees,' Iris says. 'I can feel it.' They sway. 'I can see the air coming out of your lungs, I can hear your heartbeats … and the insects in the earth, the water in all the plants.'

'Iris?' I say. They sound strange, like an echo. 'You told us where to go.' I gasp when I realise. 'The faerie bond!'

Their eyes are rolling back in their head. I scramble to them, unsure how to help but I know I have to do *something*. They have to be okay!

'Help me carry them,' the boy says.

We scoop Iris's arms over our shoulders, walking them back the way we came, towards the flowers.

'I'm sinking,' they say.

'Hang on,' I say.

We lie Iris on the ground.

I need salt. Salt is cleansing. I'm digging through our packs. 'Where is it?!' I know I packed it. Mum wouldn't have let me leave without it. 'Fuck!'

'All the worms in the earth,' Iris says. 'I can feel the water in your blood.'

'Babs?' the boy asks, tears in his eyes.

I find the salt shaker and screw off the top, my hand shaking. 'Open your mouth,' I say to Iris, but they don't understand or can't hear. Their eyes are totally white now. I grab their jaw, force their mouth open, pouring in the salt. Don't know how much is enough, have to guess. 'The stone!' I tell the boy.

He puts it in Iris's hand, curls their fingers around it.

'Come on,' I say, putting my hands over theirs. I will them to absorb whatever magic might be in the stone. 'Please.'

We sit, and we watch. Iris's breathing slows. What if they die? What if this gentle plant person ceases to exist because of me? I lock eyes with the boy, and I start crying, too. Iris can't leave, they can't.

Iris swallows, the sigil starts to glow through their shirt.

I gasp.

They slowly open their eyes and sit up.

'You okay?' the boy asks. I don't think I can speak.

'We've got to run,' they say. 'Now!'

The coldness descends on us. I can't move, but the boy and Iris take my hands, then we're running. My backpack's been left behind, but I've got the salt in my pocket. We run along the ravine and it seems to widen, wanting us to jump into its depths.

The cold fae are close. I feel their sting on my heels and cry out.

'Wait a sec,' I say as I spot more flowers in the ravine. 'Look at them.'

The others keep running, don't let me go.

'No, no, it's gotta mean something!' I let go of their hands, icy tendrils on my back. 'We have to jump!'

'*What?*' Iris yells.

'We can't run forever,' I say, and I stop running. 'Follow me!'

I jump into the ravine, my eyes never leaving the flowers. Cold air rushes through me, skewering up my flesh, my bones.

Chapter Twenty-One
The Other Side

It starts slowly, the feeling of being on the ground. At first I can sense the tips of the blades of grass against my bare legs, brushing the hairs there. The whole world smells like dirt, rich dirt. Then the firmness of the Earth creeps up, catching me from my fall, gently, curling me into itself. I lie here, being held by the planet.

I hope this was a good idea and we're not just dead.

The Earth uncurls from around me, and I start to listen. There are whipbirds, magpies, bellbirds, birds I don't recognise. There is the rustle of the wind in the leaves, the rushing of a river, and then I hear the breathing of the others, as if they were right in my ear.

When I open my eyes, slowly, blinking in the light, I see Babs and the boy spread out on the grass beside me. We're in a little clearing surrounded by ferns and rocks and forest. There are flowers, too, the witch flowers, along with hundreds of others. Closest to me I can see blue-banded bees and other native species, as well as those ones that look like bumblebees but have purple heads. 'Babs,' I say, nudging her to get her attention.

She rouses gently, coming out of the Earth's hold. 'We made it.' She sighs. 'Thanks for trusting me.'

'It's very calm here.' I look around. I can't feel the cold fae, can't feel anything out of the ordinary.

The boy sits up. 'I smell smoke, like a fireplace.'

Now that he says it, I can as well. The sun is setting through the trees, I realise, and all our things are strewn over the clearing.

'We better set up the tent,' I say, starting to stand.

I gasp. From this angle, I can see a building through the trees. It's small, made of mudbrick, tin roof.

'There's a house,' I tell the others.

'Do you think it's the witch's?' the boy asks, coming to stand beside me.

Babs stands too, and she stares at it for a while. 'Yeah.'

It doesn't feel ominous to me. It just seems like a home.

'Should we go up?' I ask.

Babs isn't sure; she starts to flicker. She looks at me with wide eyes, and I pull her into a hug. I pat the back of her head, leaning into her. 'It's okay,' I tell her. 'Why don't we just camp?'

'No, we should go see her.' Babs pulls away from the hug. 'We've come this far, and I think we have to. I have to.' She flickers once more, and then remains here. 'You want to come with me?'

'Yes,' I say, as the boy nods.

'All right.'

We leave our stuff on the ground, and Babs leads us to
the shack. As we get closer, we can smell food cooking,
something garlicky. The day gets darker quickly, and the
soft light coming from the windows is welcoming.

As I walk, I can feel the Earth hold me.

Babs creaks open the wooden gate to the garden, and
we walk up the path between rows of flowers tumbling
out of their beds. The path widens as we get closer,
bringing us in. At the front door, Babs doesn't hesitate.
She raises her hand and knocks three times, firm. She
stands tall, and waits for the knock to be answered.

There's a surprised noise from inside, and some
rustling, the clattering of pots and pans.

And then a very windblown witch opens the door. Her
black curly hair is everywhere, she has dark circles under
her eyes, and she's got a tiny piece of calcite orbiting her
head like a moon. She's wearing lots of black eyeliner,
a long, oil-slicked dark pearlescent dress, and shoes that
don't quite match. A maidenhair fern is growing out of
one of the many pockets in the dress. 'Oh,' she says, 'I'm
so glad you've returned.'

Babs is taken aback; the boy and I exchange glances.

'Come in!' The witch steps aside and gestures us
into the house. When she moves, I glimpse the open

fireplace next to a big red rug on the packed-earth floor.

We go inside. A lumpy couch and two armchairs are huddled around the fire. Dried herbs are hanging from the roof, and live healthy-looking ones are in pots along the windowsills. The plants tell me how happy they are, and they look so full of life. I relax; I think we're safe here.

'I don't know where to start,' the witch says, wringing her hands.

The boy spots a kettle on the stove. 'Maybe some tea first?'

'Good idea. Please have a seat.'

We watch as the witch starts to clean. Well, she waves a hand and the broom sweeps, while a cloth dusts down the windows. She picks a few stones off the floor and throws them into the air so they get caught in her orbit. It's mesmerising to watch them circle round and round. She is younger than I expected, maybe about thirty. Which probably means she was about twenty-five when she cursed Babs, unless witches age differently.

The couch is comfortable, and I sink in. It holds me gently, like the earth did outside.

When the kettle starts to whistle, she gets out a tea set from the cupboard, puts some loose leaves into the pot and waves a hand at the kettle, which pours its water into the pot. She rotates it a few times clockwise, muttering to herself. Then she brushes some of her wild hair off her face, walks to an armchair and sits down, and floats the tray over onto the coffee table between us. 'So,' she says, and seems unsure what to do with herself. She keeps sitting on her hands, then playing with her hair. 'How … are you? Going with it, I mean.'

'It's … interesting,' says Babs, who's been watching the witch intently the whole time.

I can sense an unbalance in Babs. She was expecting a fight, a resistance, not a woman who's just cleaned her home and made tea for some visitors.

'I knew you were like me, even though you were so small,' the witch says. 'For girls like us, it can be handy to disappear sometimes.'

'Oh.' Babs is unbalanced further still, her fire sputtering in all directions like she's in the wind. 'Oh.'

'Um, do you have a name?' the boy asks.

'For you?' the witch asks.

The boy blushes. 'I, well, I meant, what's your name?'

'Zahra,' she says. 'But I can help you find a name.'

'Oh.' He takes a big gulp of tea and seems unable to say anything else.

The fire crackles red and green. As I watch the flames, I realise two tiny creatures are in there, salamanders. They're mostly black with red and orange spots. One looks like it's sleeping on top of a log; the other is scampering through the hottest parts of the flame. And where the salamanders are, the fire is turning green. The scampering one seems to realise I'm watching it, and it goes to wake up the other one. They move behind a log where I can't see them, but I still see the green flames.

'Why did you curse me?' Babs asks Zahra softly. She flickers a couple of times, then she's gone.

Zahra stares at the space where Babs was. 'Can she hear me if I speak?'

'Yeah,' I say, 'but she can't reply. I'd wait.'

Zahra gets a red crystal chip from her pocket and balances it in her palm. She rolls it around, holding it up to the flames so the light shines through. And then she places it into her orbit. 'How long will she be gone?'

I shrug. 'Never know. But she's pretty upset, I'm guessing it'll take a while.'

'I was too headstrong when I was younger.' Zahra sighs. 'I could reverse it, if she wants.'

'Should probably wait until she's back.'

'Right.' Zahra nods. 'I suppose you two need somewhere to sleep?'

'We have a tent,' the boy says.

'It can get a bit dangerous at night here,' she says. 'I'd recommend staying inside.'

'Are the cold fae yours?' I ask, thinking of the closest danger I know.

'They aren't anyone's. But you should stay away from them, they don't mean you any good. They're angry they're stuck in this foreign land.'

'Did you make the ravine?' the boy asks.

'I did, to keep them out. But it doesn't seem to work in the night. And they're not the only dangerous things out there. Nothing can get in here, though.'

I meet the boy's eyes, and he nods.

'All right,' I say. 'But do you have room?'

'The couch folds out, and I can get another bed from somewhere …' She runs a hand through her huge hair; a fat bee flies out and perches on the nearest table. 'Oh!' She gasps and carefully picks up the bee, carries it over to what looks like a bug hotel. The bee crawls in.

A few minutes later we've cleared away the tea things, Zahra is fetching blankets, and the boy and I are sitting on the bare fold-out mattress. 'Do you reckon Babs will appear again?' he asks me. 'She won't leave?'

'Yeah, of course … I just hope she's safe. That she didn't go outside before the witch warned us about it. I wish our phones were working!'

'Maybe you can ask the plants if she's inside?'

'Hey, I never thought of that.' I go over to a pot of sage and touch one of its leaves, and it's sleepy. I close my eyes and try to feel if it knows anything about Babs. My stomach sinks.

'Well?' the boy asks when I step away from the plant.

'The sage can't feel anything. I don't know if that just means they're like us and can't see her, or if she's not here.'

I sit back on the bed just as Zahra brings us the blankets. 'I'm sure she hasn't gone outside. Don't worry too much.' She looks at me and the boy, sees our morose faces. 'Do you both like hot chocolate?'

We nod.

'All right. I'll make you some.'

As she heats a pot on the stove, the boy and I set up our double bed. Zahra has brought out a small fold-out bed for Babs, so we set that up too. The lounge room seems to grow larger so that we can fit everything in front of the fireplace for warmth. I notice the salamanders are asleep on top of the log, so maybe they've decided that we're not a threat.

Zahra hands us our mugs, turns off the lights by pointing at them, and then goes to bed with a murmured 'goodnight'. The fire grows smaller. The boy and I sit, sipping the hot chocolate that fizzes in the way Livia's and Wendy's does. It's slightly different, though; I think she's added a bit of chilli. It keeps us warm.

Thunder rumbles and rain starts to pour, very loud under the tin roof. The boy drifts off to sleep. I watch the salamanders walk all over the log, and while the fire dwindles it doesn't seem to be dying. I add another log just in case.

Something in the air shifts, and I know Babs will be back soon. My cup is still half full of warm liquid, even though I'm sure I must've drunk three cups by now.

'That smells good,' Babs says behind me.

'Hey.' I give her a big hug, trying to convey how much I care about her. 'It's really delicious. Like your mum's.'

Soon, we're sitting on the floor in front of the fire, watching the flames flick up the chimney, sharing my cup of never-ending hot chocolate. We hear a long howl outside, soon followed by another and another.

'I hope that doesn't go all night,' Babs says. 'Noisy neighbours.' She smiles, small. 'I didn't expect her to be … nice.'

'Yeah. I thought that's why you just had to go.'

'I'm not sure if I controlled it that time. It feels like I kind of did.'

'Maybe you *can* control it?'

'Maybe. I'll ask Zahra more in the morning. I reckon it's been easy to kind of hate her all this time, instead of her being someone who just wanted to help but messed up.'

'Well, I mean, you did say when you went to this house the first time you stayed here for ages, you never said anything about being captured. It sounds like you had a good time, so I guess it makes sense that she's kind. But I completely understand resenting her for cursing you. She shouldn't have done that.'

'I know. But also, it's easier to hate someone for being mean instead of realising they're just a person.'

The thunder cracks, the house shakes. Through the window, I see spindly dark shapes. I shiver and move closer to Babs. 'Cold fae outside.'

'Are we safe?'

'Zahra thinks so.'

'Hmm.' Babs takes a sip of the hot chocolate. 'Maybe she could be the magic teacher you're looking for – one who can do the kind of stuff you can.'

I don't know what to say to that, so I take another big drink of the hot chocolate. Could I have the type of power that can curse people? Do I want that? 'Maybe.'

'I mean, I wouldn't recommend going around cursing children.' Babs laughs. 'But maybe other things. The stuff she did to clean the house was pretty cool, you gotta say.'

'That would be cool. And I like her little moons.'

'They're cute. You could have some! Then Saltkin wouldn't have to keep making you special rope.'

I grip the rose quartz around my neck. 'I hope he's not too mad at me.'

'He probably will be for a bit, but I think he'll be okay in the end. He'll understand why you did it.'

'Yeah. I still should have told him.'

'Maybe nothing like this ever again without telling him first?'

I smile. 'Deal.'

Chapter Twenty-Two
The Long Walk

I wake before the others when the sun is still set. Zahra's not up either. I sit up and the only light is from the glowing coals in the fireplace. While I'm staring, a salamander pokes its head out. 'Hey,' I say, and it scampers away.

There are more logs next to the fireplace, and I grab one and chuck it on. Zahra was poking the fire last night, but I don't know how to do it and don't want to ruin the coals. Would the salamanders die? As I step away the log arranges itself anyway, flames starting up. The salamanders poke their heads up at me, so I nod at them.

The kitchen seems a lot like Mum's, with the herbs growing in little jars, the higgledy-piggledyness of it all. But there are heaps of herbs and things that Mum doesn't have. Like, there's a lot of sumac – which I only know because of the label on the jar – and about five times the amount of cinnamon sticks Mum has. There's a tiny jar with saffron inside. Mum usually can't afford actual saffron. I remember the few times she's bought it, I love looking at the strands.

The kitchen window faces into the garden, and at first I thought it was just a wild tangle of plants but it looks like it has some kind of order.

I get out my toothbrush and go in search of the bathroom. There are so many doors, too many for what seems like such a small cottage on the outside. Most are closed, but I find a library, a laundry, a room I can't see into despite using my phone torch to look inside. The bathroom's at the end of a long hallway, and I hope I can get back to the kitchen.

She has a lot of tubes and jars in the cupboard behind the mirror above the sink. Some I recognise, potions for hair and skin, but the others I'm not sure about. I open a pink sparkly jar and sniff it. It smells like musk lollies and looks like mousse. I stare at it for a second.

I shouldn't eat it.

It smells *so* good. But I screw the lid back on and put it back on the shelf.

There's a tube of toothpaste, an ordinary thing among all these awesome-looking jars, so I brush my teeth. I take a quick shower and put the same clothes back on. I stare at myself. My hair's looking sad without a fresh dye job, and I've got circles under my eyes.

What am I going to do? The witch, Zahra, she's so different to how I thought. What if she's just like me, just trying to get by in a harsh world? I knew she was trans when we first met. *Girls like us.* How did she know I was a girl, back then?

But she isn't like me – she has far more power.

I can feel the flicker of flames inside me, it wants to come back today. Maybe she could lift the curse, or ... maybe she could change it? What if I could control when I was seen and when I wasn't? I've never thought about that – I don't know if I want it gone completely.

After walking through the hallways, I finally find the kitchen again. The sun is up. I put on a jacket and go outside, though it's not really very cold. I realise I'm not wearing shoes. I wriggle my toes in the grass.

The garden has plants I recognise from the meadow and other places in the realm. Some glow with soft light, some change colours as I move. Some reach towards me, some back away. There are also herbs and flowers I know from Mum's garden. I sit on a smooth rock and watch the flowers opposite me. They reach out tendrils like snow peas. As I stick out a finger, the little vine curls around my skin.

A raven catches my eye. Have I seen it in the forest? It caws once then takes off. Maybe it's telling Vada what's going on.

I hear a door open and close. Big heavy boots on the gravel path.

Zahra's got a hat on, and a backpack over her shoulder. The coat she's wearing has about a million pockets, like her dress from last night, but this is made out of something thick like leather. Her necklaces catch in the light, shining out little rainbows. She smiles warmly, maybe sadly too, and holds up my shoes. 'Let's go for a walk.'

I lace up my shoes, and she hands me a hat that matches hers.

'How did you sleep?' she asks.

I shrug. 'Fine.'

'I thought we could go pick some veggies.'

'Okay.'

I keep sneaking glances at her while we walk. I have no idea what to say. A million things spring up, but how do I talk to someone who's made my life so lonely? Does she know? Why don't I want to tell her how much she's hurt me?

We come to a high bank covered in emerald grass and plants I don't recognise, ones with bright, luminescent leaves, and lots of grey-green mushrooms. I'm not sure what kind they are. She puts the backpack on the ground, and I realise it's made of hard wicker with a flat top. Like a big basket. 'These ones are all good, I think, just don't pick any that have weird spots. And we don't want to pick them all, only a few handfuls each.' She gets to work, throwing them into the basket as she goes.

I touch the nearest mushroom, feeling the frills underneath the head. I don't know what fish gills feel like, but maybe like this. Slightly wet, fleshy. Zahra's gripping the mushrooms from the base and just pulling them up. I do that too, surprised by how meaty they feel.

Next we go to a veggie patch in a clearing, not near her house at all. But we don't come across the vacuum of the cold fae, or any dryads, or anything else except birds and insects.

She cuts the stem of a big grey pumpkin with a fat knife and passes it to me. It feels hollow, and I cradle it in my arms.

A while later we stop at a river, and Zahra sets down the basket, now filled with veggies and herbs. I sit cross-legged and put the pumpkin in my lap while she gets out some snow peas. We crunch on them.

'I'm sorry about your curse,' she says.

'It's okay,' I say automatically.

'It's not.'

I crunch some more snow peas. 'No, it's not. You ruined my life.'

She doesn't say anything, just watches me.

'I was so lonely. It's so hard to make friends when no one can even see you! I didn't get to say goodbye to my grandma when she died because she couldn't see me. I never got to play in any team sports at school even though I'm really good at them. I can't even go to class half the time because it's too depressing to sit in a room filled with people who can't talk to you. Even with Iris and the boy – they can't see me all the time. And I need them to. I get so sad. I'm so alone.'

I'm crying. For all these years, existing without anyone seeing me. Being pushed into while walking, being overlooked in class when I know the answers or have questions.

The witch who cursed me puts a hand on my back and lets me cry.

I curl up around the pumpkin, leaning forward, blocking out the sun. I breathe in and out, big gulping breaths, letting my lungs pour out the sadness. My throat's raw by the end. She hands me a tissue and I wipe my eyes, stinging from the tears, and blow my nose.

'I can take it away, Babs. Not the years of pain, which can never be undone and I'm sorry. But the curse, I can lift it.'

I sigh. 'I don't want it gone, not all the time.'

Zahra's eyes widen. 'Really?'

'Can you help me control it?'

She smiles. 'Yes. We can rework the spell, I think.' She pulls a little worn-out book from an inside pocket of her coat and skims it. 'This might take a while.' She then gets an impossible amount of things out of her pockets: beeswax candles, little jars of herbs, crystals, paper, a golden bell, a dish. After a while, she searches through every pocket again.

'What have you lost?'

'Matches.' She sighs. 'I always forget them.'

'I'll do it.' I pick up a candle and touch the wick – it springs to life.

Zahra's face lights up in a smile. 'Thank you.'

There are seven candles, some green and some orange and a couple of white ones. She places them around me. She washes her hands in the bowl with river water and sounds the bell either side of me. I close my eyes and try to relax. She might make it worse, sure, but there's also heaps of room for growth. I think of Iris and their plants: grow.

She starts to mumble – I can't tell if it's English – and the edges of my body dissolve. I vibrate out of existence, back into it, settle in between. Though my eyes are closed, I feel colours and shapes. I even feel the sound of Zahra's voice. When she rings the bell, I see vibrations.

I don't know how long it takes. I can sense the sounds of the river and the birds and Zahra's voice, sometimes the bell. I can taste the grass under me. The fire in me roars and is subdued, roars and is subdued once more.

When the sun is in the middle of the sky, Zahra sounds the bell either side of me again. I smell the smoke of the candles and open my eyes.

She looks wrung out, her hair's even more of a mess, gumleaves are stuck in it and a little gumnut is orbiting her head, and she's sweating. But she gives me a joyful smile as she says, 'How do you feel?'

I disappear.

ALISON EVANS

When I stand up, it feels like I chose this. I feel like
I can go back, and so I reappear.

'Was that on purpose?' Zahra asks. Hope blossoms
in her eyes.

I grin, bigger than I have in my whole life. 'Yeah. I
feel great.'

Chapter Twenty-Three
The Safe Harbour

In the morning, Zahra and Babs go for a walk. At first I keep tabs on them through the plants to make sure Babs is safe, but my heart isn't in it. I know she's going to be okay. So me and the boy go grab our packs from where we left them, and then we get out things from the pantry to make breakfast. The boy cooks for us, mushrooms with balsamic vinegar on toast.

There's a light drizzle, but Zahra's got a little wooden shelter in the backyard so we sit under that. As we eat, I get a bit of a shiver. 'I wonder if I could make a fire.'

The boy shrugs. 'Probably.'

'No, I mean like, a magic fire.'

'Ohhh.' He chews for a bit, swallows. 'Probably.'

I close my eyes, concentrating on the idea of fire. I try to imagine manifesting it, but I'm too scared it'll get out of control so I stop. 'Maybe Zahra can teach me.'

The boy finishes his breakfast, places the bowl on the grass between us. 'And she said she could get me a name.'

'Yes, that sounded good.' I smile at him. 'I mean, if you want her to help.'

'I think so.' He stares off into space for a long time.

As we sit, the drizzle stops and a weak sun emerges, pale from being washed out. The garden really comes alive; bees and butterflies and other insects I don't recognise are suddenly everywhere. The boy seems to want to be alone, so I take our bowls inside. The fire is going again, the bedding cleared away, and so I sit on the rug and spread out my book. As I flick through the pages, I notice that the first few have been filled with writing.

It's an introduction. It speaks about a lot of the stuff Saltkin has told me: how magic can be dangerous and addictive, and to be careful. And it also speaks about finding your own path, the things you like and your own meanings, which is what Wendy told me about.

And then it starts to get into curses and enchantments, and goosebumps rise on my skin. The book warns about having power over others, and how this can destroy you. But I don't want power over anyone, I just want to help the world however I can, and do cool stuff like those orbiting stones.

After a few hours of reading about the elements – just how they work, not how to control them – I hear Zahra and Babs return. I suddenly feel self-conscious and try to hide my notes under the book. I copied down all the basics, drew little pictures too, and I worry that Zahra will think I don't know anything and won't want to teach me if I ask.

'Did you need lunch?' she asks as she walks through the door alone. Instead of rocks floating around her head there's a tiny gumnut. Eucalyptus leaves are tangled in her hair, though it doesn't look like that's on purpose. 'I was going to make something for the others, I'm not sure if you've eaten.'

'Yes please. Do you need help?'

'Sure.'

It doesn't take long. We make a quiche with lots of vegetables from her garden and eggs from her chickens. She has frozen pastry, and although I can't imagine her going to a supermarket, it's Homebrand, the same one sold at the Woolies near my house.

As we pop the quiche in the oven, she glances over to what I was doing before. 'Taking notes? Are you studying?'

'Um.' I blush. 'Magic.'

She looks at me deeper, her eyes searching for something that she seems to find, because she says, 'Of course.'

'I'm just beginning.'

'I can't believe the book let you find it. That's so wonderful.' She walks over to it. 'Can I look?' I nod, and I thought she meant the old book, but she picks up my notebook. I'm so nervous, my palms are sweating.

She skims through what I've written, and I can't read the look on her face. Then she sits in the closest squishy chair with the old book and props it open on her lap. The pages are about half filled for her. She flicks through, her eyes much wider than usual. 'This is amazing.' She runs a hand along the pages. 'Your notes are very thorough, too. It's good to learn the theory before the practice. Of course you don't have to. I like to.'

'Can ... can you teach me?' I ask. If she doesn't think my notes are silly, maybe we'll be okay together. 'I want to learn.'

'What about your faeries?' she asks, head cocked to one side.

'How do you know about them?'

'The rope around your neck.' She points to where it hangs under my shirt. 'That wasn't made by humans.'

I take hold of the rose quartz. 'Saltkin gave me this stone, too.'

She smiles. 'I can tell.'

'Do you know any faeries?'

She shakes her head. 'Not really. I think because I don't stay in the same place for very long, so it's hard to get to know anyone.'

'What about your salamanders?'

'Apart from them.' She's looking fondly over towards the fireplace.

'So does that mean the place your house is built on moves to different areas? Or it exists somewhere else?'

'Well, it's always somewhere else. I guess the ... doors, so to speak, they appear in different areas. The door in your forest is how you got here, that's a new one.'

'So.' I chew my lip. 'If you move a lot, does that mean maybe you shouldn't be my teacher?'

'Maybe not forever, but I could be for a while,' she says gently. 'And maybe that door can stay for longer than I would normally let it – there are many doors, you know.'

'Right.'

She hands me the book and my notes. 'This is such a good guide. I wish I had this when I was younger! It'll help so much. And if it let you find it, you must be able to do amazing things. With the right training, of course.'

'Saltkin said magic can be very addictive, and so does the introduction to the book.'

'It can be, especially for humans. When I cursed Babs, I was at a stage where I thought I could just do whatever I wanted with my powers. But we have to remember, it's not up to us to change anyone's lives, unless they ask. And even then it can be tricky.'

My eyebrows come together in a frown. 'What if it was to do good?'

'But then what is good? I thought I was doing Babs a favour, but it meant she couldn't make friends until you.'

I want to ask about cursing people for doing bad things, out of revenge.

'And no, I don't do revenge curses, or for justice. I used to, and it never ends well. It always finds a way to come back to you.' She smiles sadly. 'A lot of people will start to avoid you, as well – not from cursing, just from being a magic user. They'll feel something is different about you, and they'll turn away.'

'Everyone?'

'Not everyone. But it may happen more often with strangers than you'd think.'

'Does that happen with you a lot?'

'Yes.'

'Is that why you live alone?'

'I just prefer this. Babs was telling me about her mother, a witch who does live near the town, but she's reclusive as well. Then there's the woman who runs the cafe you go to. Magic has nothing to do with where I live. It just makes it easier for me to get completely away.'

The kitchen timer goes off, and I get Babs and the boy to come in for lunch. Babs looks tired, and after we finish eating she folds out the double-bed mattress and lies down. The boy wants to speak with Zahra in private, so I decide to take a shower finally, after who knows how long of walking through the forest.

Then I see the bath: big and deep with clawed feet that stretch out over the grey pebbled floor. A pouch of herbs hangs from the spout, and I smell it; it's got lavender and salt and other herbs I don't recognise. It hums peacefully as I hold it. I'm sure Zahra won't mind if I have a bath, so I start to run one. The herb pouch turns the water a deep, shimmering purple that swirls with blue. My whole body relaxes.

I dip in my foot and it's the right temperature. So I jump in. As I close my eyes and let my head go under water, air bubbles tickle over my skin as they rise. The bath is somehow the perfect shape for me, and as I lie there, sunlight streaming into the room, the water stays the perfect temperature. Then I can't feel the tub anymore; it's just like the other time when my bath seemed to turn into a river. When my head breaks the surface, the bath has grown blue waterlilies. A dragonfly hovers before buzzing away. I can hear a frog but I can't see it.

I take the rope with the rose quartz off my neck and hold it just above the water. I try to focus on it, to make it revolve around my head, but nothing happens. Maybe it's too advanced, or maybe I need something else. I look down at the sigils etched onto my skin, and the tattoo the boy poked into me. So much has happened these past weeks, I don't know how much can fit inside the rest of the year.

I trace the protection sigil on my chest, and I let it power down. For a moment I expect cold fae to come tearing in, but we're safe here. Perhaps at night I'll activate it again, but for now I think it's okay to let it relax.

The bath stretches out to fill the whole room. A river forms. There are more dragonflies, more lilies, some swamphens even. Then all kinds of birds and insects and plants, and I float in the middle of it, supported, feeling as if I am the whole of this world I've created somehow with this bath. I see a kingfisher fly over, and a couple of black swans in the distance.

I don't know how long I stay there; it feels like hours.

When I go out into the lounge, Zahra and the boy are still outside, and Babs is still half asleep. I curl up over her, wrapping my arm around her waist.

'How are you?' Babs asks me, her voice sticky from sleep.

I yawn, my eyes heavy. 'The bath turned into a pond.'

'Mm.' She curls tighter. 'Zahra tried to shift my curse, so I can control it easier.'

'Did you ask her to take it away?'

'I thought about it.'

I press my ear to her back and I can feel her heartbeat, flickering like the logs in the fireplace. Although it shouldn't be yet, the sun is setting. The salamanders have come out.

'I don't think I wanted her to take it away, anyway.' Babs yawns. 'It's who I am. And besides, maybe it'll come in handy. Hey, it already comes in handy – I can *not* go to school whenever I want.' She laughs, her body rumbling against mine. 'I don't think I want to get rid of it completely.'

'That makes sense.' My body is so heavy, I'm ready to

melt into the mattress. Everything's so warm.

The boy crawls in behind me. He doesn't spoon me like I'm spooning with Babs, but he's there and I can feel his warmth. 'I think we found a name,' he says.

'Oh?' I say.

Babs and I turn around so we can see him in the gentle light from the fireplace. We're all sitting up, now.

'My name is Hasim.' He sits a little taller, puffs his chest out the tiniest bit.

Babs and I grin at him.

'That's perfect,' she says, and we're both pulled into a hug.

Hasim can't stop smiling.

'This calls for a celebration,' I say, and go over to the stove where I find the hot chocolate has already been warmed up. I pour us all mugs, and we clink them together and toast to Hasim's name, Babs's control over her curse, and my new teacher.

We're finally heading back home. It's been days, I think, and I know we should have left already. But it's so peaceful here, the island of magic where Zahra lives. We help her with the garden, and cooking, and she teaches me magic.

I'm still a long way off being able to have an orbit, or to get the broom to sweep the house, but I can make protection spells and good luck charms, little things that can help people. Some more book pages have been revealed, and I have a few more sigils on me as well. The first ones are fading a bit, though they still glow when I activate them.

'You know you'll be able to come back any time,' Zahra says, as we strap on our backpacks. She's done a spell to make them lighter, and she taught me how to do it.

'I'll see you in a few weeks,' I tell her as we hug, and she nods. We're going to meet regularly so I can keep learning, and she'll read more of the book while I'm there as well. I know I'll have to get permission from Clover and Moss, but I'm sure it will work out.

'Be safe,' Zahra says. 'I've made the door come out into your backyard, Babs.'

Then Zahra hugs Babs and Hasim, and gives us all some food for the journey, just in case it takes longer than we think.

As we walk the short distance to the door, we don't speak. I reach out a hand, and the space beyond the door feels like salt water, cool and calming. I feel sad, leaving the witch and her haven, but I miss my mothers, and they'll be worried about me.

We step through the door, and the Earth comes up to meet us.

Chapter Twenty-Four
The Journey Home

The portal leads us right into my garden. Mum sees us from the kitchen window and she comes outside, drying her hands on a tea towel. She's frowning. 'Are you all right?' she asks, pulling me into a hug. 'Why are you back so soon?'

'We've been gone for ages,' I say, frowning at her. 'A week, maybe more.'

Wendy shakes her head. 'Not here, I almost just said goodbye to Iris. I was doing our breakfast dishes.' She holds up her tea towel.

I laugh, because it's so strange. 'We'll tell you all about it.' I didn't realise the time difference would be so much – I couldn't remember it clearly enough.

We go inside, Hasim makes a pot of Earl Grey, and we all have lunch except Mum because she's just eaten. She nods all the way through our story, holding my hand, sometimes asking questions but mostly just listening. At the end she says, 'I'm glad you're okay.' She sighs. 'I wanted to stop you, but I didn't want you to have to sneak away, Babs.'

I nod. 'Yeah. But I had to go.'

'I know. I'm glad you got back safe.'

Hasim and Iris look at each other, and I know they're thinking they should go.

I notice something behind Iris as the three of us are saying goodbye at the front door. It's sparkling, and I realise it's Saltkin.

'Hey, Saltkin,' Iris says, looking at the ground.

'Hi, sprout,' he says. 'I'm glad you're safe. I wanted to thank your friends for helping with the bond when it broke. I was worried, but I knew you'd be able to handle it together.'

Hasim and I look at each other, unsure of what to say.

'We just ... had to. You don't need to thank us,' I say eventually. Hasim nods with me.

Iris holds out their hand, and Saltkin sits on it this time. Iris says, 'Sorry I lied to you.'

'Thank you.' He pats their palm. 'Please don't do it again.'

'I won't.'

He smiles. 'You'll have to tell me all about your adventure with the witch.'

'Her name is Zahra and she's going to be my teacher!' Iris says with a grin. 'She was impressed by the book.' Iris and Saltkin wave goodbye and walk off together, still chatting.

'What am I gonna tell my dad?' Hasim asks. 'About why we're home so early.'

I look up at the sky. It's metal-grey and more clouds are rolling in, but it's not raining yet. 'Maybe we cancelled the trip because it's going to rain … maybe it'll rain heaps?'

He smiles. 'All right. Well, see you Monday.'

At school on Monday, the teachers remind us that the term is ending soon, and that we have exams coming up, and all that kind of stuff. It's stressful, and I'm worried I won't be able to stay. I make it to science class and lunchtime. Last class of the day is art, always the hardest, but something tells me I can do it.

The three of us walk into the room together, and I stay.

We take our seats on one of the big square tables, and get out our sketchbooks, and I'm still here. My warmth bubbles up into the whole room.

Miranda doesn't give us a spiel about how term is ending, she just tells us to keep going with our projects, and that she'll be coming around to check in.

I've decided to use mostly watercolours, then Iris will help enchant the page so it shimmers. The glitter I tried to apply always looked wrong, like it wasn't quite real. But if I infuse the paper with magic, surely I can make it work. They're going to do the same thing, and Hasim as well. Our projects won't look the same, but like three of a set.

Miranda comes around, gives Iris some pointers. I think what they've got looks amazing, watercolours and shining light. Hasim tells Miranda that that's his name now, and she uses it several times without making it seem forced. And when she gets to me, she brings out some references of geometrical patterns from a book and finds the perfect one. It almost matches my first tattoo design, the one from before I got the rose.

'These are all looking really good, you three,' she says, and she smiles that genuine smile of hers. Even though we're only average at art, I think it's our favourite class now.

As art class ends, I feel a bit lighter. We separate to get our bags from our lockers, then we meet out the front of school to go down to Eaglefern.

Livia hugs me when we walk in. 'I was so worried,' she says. 'Your mum told me what was happening. And you two!' She takes their hands. 'You're very brave.'

Hasim and Iris look like they don't really know how to respond. He shrugs, they smile.

We get our drinks and sit on the couches. The

flowerboxes now take up almost half the window, and the blue bees look even bigger.

'So I was thinking,' I say, after our drinks arrive, 'we should probably go camping for real in the summer holidays once school is done. We can go to this place Mum took me to a couple times. There's a cave you can explore, and a river nearby, and it's gotta be magic, I swear.'

'That sounds nice,' Hasim says, smiling softly.

'I've always wanted to explore a cave!' Iris says.

As the two of them talk through the logistics – who has what, if we need to get another tent, how long to go for – I smile at them. I can feel the warmth of them both in my bones, and I know it'll be the best summer.

Acknowledgments

This book was written on the stolen lands of the Wurundjeri and Boon Wurrung people of the Kulin Nation. Sovereignty was never ceded. I pay my respects to Elders past, present and emerging.

I am an uninvited guest on these lands and waters. The homes I have lived in have been on the lands of the Wurundjeri and Boon Wurrung people. I grew up in the Dandenong Ranges and you can take a cultural tour to learn more about the area, see wurundjericulturaltours.com.au.

A lot of people go into the writing of a book. Since releasing my first YA, *Ida*, I have been welcomed into the #loveozya community. A huge thanks goes to Sarah and Alex for having *Ida* as their first book of the month for The YA Room, and thanks to Sarah, Shaun and Bianca for their ongoing support.

To any teen who has come up to me after an event to thank me, or to get a book signed, I remember all of you. And to the ones who quietly read, who I will never meet, thank you. It is an honour to write for you all, and

I cannot express how much it means to me to hear that my books have helped you. It is a privilege to write for you. Thank you thank you thank you.

YA authors are very kind people, and I would like to thank Lili Wilkinson, Cally Black, Marlee Jane Ward, Nicole Hayes, Jodi McAlister, Katya de Becerra, Amie Kaufmann, Leanne Hall, Jes Layton, Jordi Kerr, Jess Walton, Rafeif Ismail, Alec Te Pohe, Carolyn Gilpin, Erin Gough, Michael Earp and Michael Pryor in particular. And while they are not necessarily YA authors, I would like to thank Katherine Back, Rae White, Benjamin Law, Amelia Lush and Gene Smith. Everyone on this list is inspiring, thank you for your dedication. You've taught me a lot. Thank you for the friendship, the kindness, and the help. Even if we have only spoken a handful of times, or rarely see each other, you're appreciated.

Two books showed me that I could write a book like this one; *Night Swimming* by Steph Bowe and *Fairytales for Wilde Girls* by Allyse Near. Thank you both for writing these beautiful books.

I would like to thank Nevo Zisin in particular – I am so glad we found each other. Your friendship means so much and has healed me in a way I didn't know I needed to be healed. Working with you, writing stories and being on panels together has been the highlight of my career, and I'm truly grateful we are friends.

Thank you to the bookstagrammers, the reviewers, the bloggers, and the vloggers of the YA community.

You all put in so much work. The community is strong because of you.

"Dear Reader" is a direct influence of my Queerstories speech "World School" from July 2018, which I wrote while writing the beginnings of *Euphoria Kids*. Thank you to Maeve Marsden for asking me to be a part of the event, it helped me articulate a lot of what I want to do with my work.

To my mum, my brother, my Nanna and Grumps, and all the hundreds of other Evanses, thank you for being a wonderful, kind, thriving family. I am very lucky to be with you all.

Thank you to Joni, my fiancee and soon-to-be wife. Thank you for being my first reader, for your edits, ideas, questions, and answers.

The Echo team – I couldn't have done any of this without you. Liz, thank you for the first edit of *Euphoria Kids* that helped me find the real starting point. Although we rarely see each other, thank you to Benny and Sandy, for all your work behind the scenes that I don't see, but I know you work so hard. Thanks Brendan for your email updates and excellent highlighting system, having you in my corner is amazing and I feel so lucky. Thank you to Shaun for making my words look beautiful again, and for hanging out with me at other Echo book launches. Thank you to Jo Hunt for another amazing cover design, and thank you to Jem Bradbrook for the illustration that is more wonderful than I could have dreamed. And Kate, where would this story be without you. Thank you for all your advice and gentle but firm direction, and for staying up with me until the wee hours of the morning.

And finally, thank you to Angela Meyer, who by the time this book is released, will be on a new journey. You have been a wonderful editor, publisher and friend. This book would not be here if it weren't for you. You have continually made a safe space for me to make art and I have adored working with you. Thank you for believing in me and my work, thank you for your endless support, and thank you for helping me grow as a person and a writer. I can't wait to see what you do next.

ALSO BY ALISON EVANS

IDA

Winner of People's Choice Award at the
Victorian Premier's Literary Awards 2018

How do people decide on a path, and find the drive to
pursue what they want?

Ida struggles more than other young people to work this
out. She can shift between parallel universes, allowing her
to follow alternative paths.

One day Ida sees a shadowy, see-through doppelganger of
herself on the train. She starts to wonder if she's actually
in control of her ability, and whether there are effects far
beyond what she's considered.

How can she know, anyway, whether one universe is
ultimately better than another? And what if the continual
shifting causes her to lose what is most important to her,
just as she's discovering what that is, and she can never
find her way back?

Ida is an intelligent, diverse and entertaining novel that
explores love, loss and longing, and speaks to the condition
of an array of overwhelming, and often illusory, choices.

Learn more: echopublishing.com.au